JUST A TICK OF WHIMSY

VOLUME 1

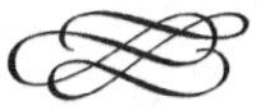

B. A. PAUL

CONTENTS

FOREWORD

What do Wonder Woman, Mr. Rogers and an unnamed teenage girl I met playing in a creek bed down the road from my childhood home have in common?

They all became fixtures in the imaginary universe I created when I was young.

Call it boredom. Call it only-child syndrome. Call it psychosis.

Call it whatever, but those figures (some borrowed from others' creations and some all my very own), spent countless hours with me padding around after my Boston terriers, lazing in my room or swinging—alone, but not alone—on the rickety metal playset in my backyard. You know, those old swing sets where that one pole always left the ground once the swing hit a certain elevation, twisting the entire top support beam into a squealing pretzel…

A precursor to that epic space adventure I scribbled, these characters would come and go as I needed them. I was the center of their universe. How cool is that? Mr. Rogers and his entire neighborhood gang all mine—right down to the mailman. All mine to have whatever adventure I could muster—including a trip to the Crayola Crayon Factory through his magic Picture Picture.

And Wonder Woman never had to use her lasso of truth on Mr.

Rogers—only on the rotten kids from my class that would also show up in the yard or in the living room. She'd kick their bully butts and we'd be off to lasso up another adventure. Superman showed up occasionally, too. Wonder Woman constantly had to save his rear end from the first-grade bully bearing the kryptonite crayon. (See any themes to my madness?)

Adventures. Day in and day out.

Alone, but not alone.

I can only imagine (no pun intended) what kind of adventures I would have had back then if the Marvel movies of today played in theaters in the '80s. [And I just deleted two paragraphs of wonderful what-ifs to file away for another writing session. Although, now that I understand copyright infringement better than my six-year-old counterpart, I'll proceed carefully.]

Looking back, I know my parents must have seen me talking to myself. Or maybe they thought I was singing to the pudgy Boston pups who were never far from my heels. They had to know, right?

But I distinctly remember the day I knew I'd been "caught."

My dad built our house, and he routinely did maintenance on the place himself. On this particular day, he was running wire or plumbing or something in the crawlspace. He took me into the dusky damp underbelly of the house with him, and I got to take my own hot pink flashlight. (The things we remember…)

The access to the crawlspace was through a small, partial basement the size of a closet that always had about a foot of water at the bottom. He dropped a ladder in as there were no stairs, leaned it against the wall, and once he was set, he one-armed me through the air, over the mini pond, and through the access door. The space was big enough for me to walk hunched over. I handed him some tools as he slithered on his belly and tinkered with the project. Then he dismissed me to explore.

Imagination fodder! Before I became claustrophobic.

The nameless girl from the creek I'd met a few weeks before showed up in the crawlspace. (I'm not quite sure why I latched onto her so tightly. She was kind and played with me—a real person, to splash and be splashed with, maybe—but I named her Alice and we had great times together though I never actually saw her again.)

Then Wonder Woman appeared. I got miffed at Alice for hogging all the attention, since it was Alice's own stupid fault she got herself stuck between the floor joists and needed rescue. Superman showed up—in the form of Clark—to settle things diplomatically. My pink flashlight lit the corners and crannies with a pale yellow beam, showing the characters where to go and what to do next.

And then it happened.

"Who are you talking to?"

I froze. I remember that heart-stopping sensation where the seconds don't move. My dad was incredibly intimidating most of the time, so I wasn't sure if I was in trouble. Lie or tell the truth?

Lie.

"No one." Well, maybe it wasn't a lie. There was no one there.

Truth.

"Sounds like it was someone." I whipped my flashlight toward him, he scolded me for shining it in his eyes, but he was grinning. My heart started beating again and I turned back toward the corner where just seconds before Alice had gotten hung on the floor above us.

Diana Prince, Clark Kent, Alice.

Gone.

Alone.

I tried to be careful from then on. I realized talking out loud meant letting others afford a small peek behind the curtain—a curtain I didn't want real people to look behind. Because it was *mine.* I think I held on to that world a little longer than most kids. My daughter's imaginary friends (a boy named Tyler and B.I. the cat) moved out after she started preschool. My son never had any that he let me know about.

Maybe I eased into writing that epic space story as a way to add layers to a universe where I could control things. I could stop talking to myself and eliminate the risk of getting "caught." (Though, as I age, I find that I'm talking to myself at an increasingly alarming frequency, but at least it's to *myself,* not Clark Kent…or Tony Stark.)

I could write in solitude for as long as I wished. Alone, but not alone.

Call it boredom. Call it only-child syndrome. Call it psychosis.

Call it whatever, but the drive to create and write (and, yes, to control something in an otherwise uncontrollable and unpredictable life) still burns inside me. At any given moment, I have entire paragraphs of dialog running in my mind with descriptions of settings, beats of action and twisted plots.

And that little girl with the hot pink flashlight is having a blast again.

Occasionally my inner critic will boom out, "Who are you talking to?" The voice that threatens to halt heartbeats and freeze time.

So I summon Wonder Woman to kick butt.

And I move on.

Alone in my thoughts. But never alone…

Happy reading!

B. A. Paul

THE RAVEN

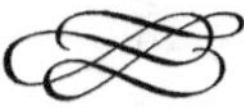

After taking a voluntary layoff to spend more time at home with his daughter, Craig finds himself more and more unsettled by the young girl's insistence on spending time with her imaginary friends. His wife thinks he's merely being paranoid, but there's something strange about Tamara, and the things her friends tell her to do...

Craig Edwards took a voluntary layoff from the company he'd founded two months ago. The former CEO of a thriving business, now playing role of stay-at-home daddy and chauffer to Tamara, his eight-year-old daughter, so his wife could earn enough to keep the electric on. It was easier for Marsha to jump back into the workforce after a quick renewal of her CNA license than for him to find comparable income doing anything else while his company got back on track.

What surprised Craig was that Marsha seemed all too eager for the change. She didn't flinch or complain about leaving the house for twelve-to-fourteen-hour shifts.

Understanding replaced the surprise once he'd survived his first full week at home with his daughter, the love of his life—or so the dozen photo frames in his office had indicated. If Craig were honest with himself, Tamara had been simply a little girl he'd thrown a few hours at when it was convenient for him. He'd tried to connect with her over the years, but the bond just hadn't formed. At one time, Craig had lost many nights of sleep comparing his daughter's affection for him to that of other little girls with their dads he'd see at the playground or the school parking lot at drop-off times. Craig and Tamara just hadn't connected.

Something was different about her—she seemed disconnected to the point of melancholy.

Craig didn't lose sleep over it anymore. He just took it at face value. There were other matters to keep him up nights.

The first week at home, which happened to be the first week of summer vacation, was harder than any week at the office by a long shot. Since Marsha would fall into bed shortly after coming home, Craig took on Tamara's care and the upkeep of the house—all those chores he'd gladly left to his wife for their eleven years of marriage.

The fourteenth day into Marsha's new job and Craig's new existence, he stayed up through the night, working feverishly at the dining room table where he laid out their budget, upcoming bills, computer-printed copies of blank calendars for the next three months, and a notepad for any random brilliant idea that might strike him.

Any idea brilliant enough to get him behind his desk and get Marsha home with their child.

He shuffled papers and bills from one pile to the next. Electric. Medical. The therapy bills were the worst, because neither he nor his wife could see any real progress in Tamara.

He sighed, rubbed his neck and stood to stretch. He really did love them both. No one could ever take Marsha's place. And Tamara had been an absolute joy until she'd turned three. Marsha noted she'd walk around in a world with her imaginary friends. The friends would tell her to do things, and she'd obey them or "help" them carry out whatever cockamamie plan they desired, often to the detriment of household appliances, the dog, and Marsha's prized photo albums.

Looking back, Craig hadn't taken any of it too seriously and had told Marsha their daughter would likely grow out of it once she started making real friends. That's what had happened to Craig. He'd outgrown Smithers as soon as Robby Harver moved in down the street from him. The imaginary walrus had waddled after Craig far less often once the friendship with Robby grew. And Smithers never came back once Craig started first grade.

Nostalgia punched him in the gut. Smithers and he had had some grand adventures in his back yard and at the playground. And where on earth did a four-year-old come up with the name Smithers?

Where had his daughter ever heard the odd names she'd given to her invisible pals?

He and Marsha had decided not to tell their daughter about Smithers. The therapist agreed. With their child's level of intensity, it might fuel the fire they so desperately wanted to put out.

The punch was replaced by a chill. Things were far more intense with Tamara than he could ever have dreamed.

Over the last few days, Craig had received a hefty dose of Samson and Twila and Leo. Craig asked Tamara what her friends looked like, what they liked to eat, and even if they'd like to go with her and Craig to see a movie. He'd tried his hardest to connect with her and, hopefully, talk some sense into her. Other eight-year-olds seemed to have a life outside of their own heads. Not Tamara.

All she'd given him was that one looked like an ant, one a honey bee, and one a spider. And no, they didn't want people food. And—after Tamara had held an emergency meeting with the three friends—no, neither they nor she cared to visit the movie theater. When Craig had asked if she wanted to invite any girls from her class to come and play, she said Leo was too shy and Samson was a "hater," so it wouldn't be a good idea.

Craig couldn't keep the names straight with the characters, even though Tamara had told him several days in a row. Yesterday, the day that had prompted Craig's all-nighter in the dining room, he'd gotten the ant's name wrong, and Tamara had flown to pieces, tossing family photos off the entryway table, busted glass shattering on the tile. She'd stomped upstairs and slammed the door so hard that the casing splintered at the door latch.

When he'd explained what had happened to Marsha that evening, all she had offered was a sad smile and a nod of the head before she'd collapsed onto the couch in exhaustion, where she'd stayed all night. Working double shifts at the nursing home was easier than dealing with the daily life of their daughter.

He slumped over the table. He should have been more help to Marsha with this. Maybe if he'd spent more time with them, this imaginary friend thing wouldn't have escalated so badly.

He shuffled the papers around on the table as dawn broke through the front windows, waking Marsha. She rose from the fetal position, stretched and wiped her eyes. He joined her on the couch.

"We need to talk."

"Good morning to you, too." She leaned over to kiss him, then held his face in both of her hands. "What happened to you?"

"I was up all night." He laid the months of June, July and August in her lap. He'd crossed out one week and three days from June's boxes. Days he'd just barely survived. "Working on this."

"What is this?" She flipped through the months. August 31st boasted a red star.

"That's the date I plan to go back to work."

She let the pages fall to her lap. "How's that?"

He took her hands. "Marsha, I can't take this. Tamara needs you. I'm no good for her. I'm no good around here. I'm barely able to keep things running. I need to work. By then, with me taking no salary, the company will be stronger. I won't go back with full benefits, but I'll—"

"What if I don't want you to? Tamara's fine. It's only been a few weeks. You'll get used to it."

"I don't think so, Marsha." He stood and looked out the window. "I *need* to go back."

"What about *my* job?"

"What about it? You come home more tired than you were if you'd been home all day. Tamara misses you."

"Don't use her like that. And I like what I'm doing. It's a good kind of tired."

"You'll be able to quit right as school starts. You'll have some time for yourself."

Marsha stood and flung a pillow at his head. "This isn't about me. Don't pretend. This is you, doing what you do, being selfish and avoiding your daughter." She stomped upstairs and Craig heard the shower start.

Three seconds later Tamara was at the top of the stairs and his heart sank to his toes. He hoped she hadn't heard the words Marsha hurled at him.

"I'm hungry, Daddy," Tamara said as she wobbled sleepily down the steps toward the dining room table. She walked with her palm out in front of her, as if she were holding something. Probably Samson.

Maybe Twila. Who knew?

"I'll be right there." Craig picked up the calendar pages scattered over the floor. He took them to the kitchen and hung them on the refrigerator. He used a permanent marker to draw a fat line through the eleventh day of June. Today.

He'd go back to work if it killed him.

~

MARSHA ATE WITH TAMARA, gave her a hug and kiss, and then she kissed the imaginary being in Tamara's palm. The little girl giggled and ran off upstairs. Marsha left for the hospital after asking Craig whether she even had a say in the family anymore. He didn't feel like getting into it, so he remained silent.

Craig cleaned up the breakfast mess and was about to put the milk in the fridge when he noticed June and July's boxes were all marked through—some neatly, like his marks, some squiggly and some zig-zaggy. Tamara.

It really wasn't a big deal, but now he'd have to print off new calendars and relocate the marker. He took them off the fridge and went to Tamara's room.

Tamara was sitting at her pink wooden tea table set for four. The blue and yellow porcelain set had been a gift from his mother a few years ago. She poured and served up imaginary goodies daily, sometimes three or four times a day.

"Hey, sweetheart." Craig tried to tread carefully. He didn't want a repeat of the other day with the glass and the door.

"Hi, Daddy. Want some tea?"

He smiled and brushed the brown locks from her face. "No, sweetheart. I'm all full of milk and coffee."

She nodded and went back to what she was doing.

"Did you do this to Daddy's calendars?"

She glanced up at the papers in his hand and nodded. "Yes."

"Why? Tamara, I'm not mad, but I'd like to know why you did it. They aren't yours to mark on. If you'd like to color, I'd be happy—"

"No, Daddy. I didn't want to color. Jefferson told me to do it." She poured more imaginary tea and shuffled the saucers on the table.

Craig sat down on the floor next to Tamara's chair. Another one. Another "friend" to blame things on. Very carefully, as if not to awaken a sleeping giant, he asked, "Who's Jefferson?"

"He's new. He came yesterday."

"And what does Jefferson like to do?" Craig tried to form his questions very carefully. Not judgmental. Not unbelieving. Just careful.

"He's a black bird with a white face. Like he dipped it into paint or something, but it's not paint. It's feathers. And he likes to tell me things. And he wants to tell you things, too. And he told me to mark those papers." She stopped fiddling with the tea set and looked Craig straight in the eye. "Because you can't go back to work, Daddy. Jefferson said."

Craig faltered. Not because he believed her, but because now he knew she had heard the fight with Marsha earlier this morning. Maybe she was feeling the effects of his job loss and her mom's absence and this was her way of acting out. Her way of resisting change.

"Sweetheart, that's nothing for you to worry about. Let Mommy and Daddy worry about the grownup stuff, and you just worry about kid stuff, okay?"

"So you won't go back?"

Craig stood up and lifted Tamara into his arms from the tiny chair —the one she'd outgrown two years ago. She wrapped her arms around his neck for the first time in a long time and squeezed. "How about instead of worrying about Daddy's work, we go on a Daddy-daughter date?"

She looked over her shoulder at the three empty seats, then back to Craig with sad brown eyes.

"The whole gang can come to the matinee. I'll even buy them popcorn." He poked her in the stomach and she giggled. "Or they can stay here and it can be just us."

She looked back over her shoulder, thought for a moment and smiled. "They said it was okay. We can go, just us." She wriggled out of his arms and took off downstairs.

"Gee guys. Thanks for letting her have the afternoon off. I really appreciate it." Craig tipped an imaginary hat to the imaginary tea guests, gathered his marked-up calendars, and chased after Tamara.

THE LAST FEW hours with the movie and a fast food meal had been the best Craig had spent with Tamara all summer. Maybe even for the last couple of years. They'd laughed and giggled. She'd even tolerated a romp through the park, up and down the slide a few times, and let him push her on the swings.

She never mentioned an imaginary friend. Not once. She did, a couple of times, gaze out the window or up to the sky and seemed to drift off, but she came back quickly and engaged with Craig easily.

This was what he'd longed for. What he'd given up on. Maybe he'd move the therapy bills to the top of the pile. Pay them first.

His glee was short-lived. Back home, she raced upstairs to "check on the gang" and Craig feared he may have lost her for the rest of the day. It did give him time to print out a new calendar set and mark off the eleven days. This time, he kept them in the spare-bedroom office on his desk. It would be less traumatic that way for both Tamara and Marsha, but would still give Craig the visual motivation he needed to survive woman's work and the ins and outs of Tamara for the next few months.

Marsha would be home in a few hours. As a peace offering, he decided to vacuum and get dinner started early. He checked on Tamara—back at the tea table—and went on with the chores.

About an hour before Marsha was due, he went to his office to tuck away the calendars, just in case she'd happen to come across them and the fight would start all over again. He'd drop the subject for a while and let things cool off.

The calendars weren't on the corner where he'd left them. He looked all over the room, but they weren't there. He went down the hall to Tamara's room, where she was sprawled on the floor, coloring.

"Tamara, did you see Daddy's calendars?"

Without looking at Craig, she fished the papers from underneath her coloring book and held them in the air.

He took them from her. Every square on all three pages was colored, marked through or crossed out. Except for August 31st. That one had been ripped off the page altogether.

He knelt beside his daughter. "Tamara, look at me."

She rolled over on her back and looked up at Craig.

"Why did you do this again?"

"Jefferson warned me. He said you can't go back to work. You need to just throw those papers away, Daddy."

"I don't want you to touch Daddy's things, okay? If there's something in my office, that means it doesn't belong to you. You can't color on these anymore."

"I don't want to color on them. Jefferson warned me that you can't go back."

"Okay, okay." The last thing he needed was for Tamara to be in a fit when Marsha got home.

"Just don't go back, and then Jefferson won't be mad." Tamara stood up, and Craig feared she'd escalate to a tantrum if he didn't think of something quickly.

"Hey, I'd like to meet Jefferson. It seems like he's a pretty smart guy." Tamara's shoulders relaxed, and so did Craig's. "Do you think I could meet him?" Craig looked around the room.

Tamara smiled. "He's not in here, silly. He's a bird."

"Oh, okay." Craig pulled back the white lace curtain and looked out Tamara's window. The oak in the front yard needed trimming; the branches were almost brushing the front of the house.

"See? There he is." Tamara was at his elbow, pointing.

Craig barely caught sight of a black bird, whether white-faced or not Craig couldn't tell. It flew away before he could focus on it.

"Oh, Daddy, you scared him. Maybe tomorrow." Tamara went back to the coloring books.

"Maybe tomorrow." Craig went back to the kitchen to finish cooking.

Dinner proceeded peacefully. He apologized to Marsha for springing such an important decision on her the way he'd done. They promised to talk about it when they weren't so exhausted. Tamara chimed in here and there with news of Twila and the newcomer, Jefferson.

After tucking Tamara in, Marsha managed to make it to the bedroom before she fell into an exhausted heap. Craig went to the office and closed the door.

He printed off the third set of summer months, marked off the

June days, circled August 31st in red, and filed all of them in his bottom desk drawer.

He fell into bed next to Marsha, equally exhausted but determined to connect with Tamara again and not let the house fall down tomorrow.

THE MORNING STARTED AS PEACEFULLY as dinner had ended. Marsha was off to work, Tamara ate breakfast and disappeared upstairs, and Craig started cleaning up the mess. The first chance he got, he headed upstairs, peeked in on his daughter, and went to the office. He pulled the bottom file drawer open and removed the calendars.

"You have got to be kidding me!"

He stomped down the hall to Tamara's room.

"Again? Jefferson or not, imaginary friends or not, Tamara, I want you to stop this!"

Craig's volume startled Tamara to tears.

"Daddy, he made me. He said you can see him, but you can't go. He says I need you to stay here with me and help me!"

"Enough, Tamara!"

"But Daddy, look!" Tears streaked her face, and she pointed to the window.

He pulled back the lace curtains and dropped the calendars on the floor. On the branch nearest the window sat a black bird with a white head, staring directly into the bedroom. The bird didn't flinch, except to shift its gaze from Craig to Tamara and back again.

"Hi! Jefferson." Tamara wiped her tears on the sleeve of her T-shirt and rushed to the window.

The bird still didn't move.

"This is my Daddy. Daddy, this is Jefferson."

Craig wasn't sure what to do, so he did nothing.

"You see him, right Daddy?" Tamara looked up with hopeful eyes.

Craig nodded and found his voice and turned to his daughter. "Yes, I see him. He's a very strange-looking bird, for sure, but that doesn't mean he's telling you to ruin Daddy's papers." This was nonsense. She'd made up an imaginary friend on the wings of this bird and was using him to misbehave.

"You're gonna make him mad. He says he doesn't want you to go to work." She pointed to the bird.

Craig ignored her urges and was about to explain why lying and making up stories was a bad deal when he heard tapping.

"He says you're special, like me!"

He turned to see the bird, hovering clumsily in mid-air, pecking at the window. He flung his arms at the creature, and it finally flew off.

"He says you're special like me!" Tamara shrieked and ran downstairs, leaving a wake of slammed doors and toppled and broken décor in her path.

Craig couldn't take it anymore. Nature itself was against him having a peaceful existence with his daughter. Even after the great afternoon they'd had yesterday, Craig had had enough. He dialed Marsha's cell and was surprised when she picked up.

"You've got to come home. She's out of control." Tamara screamed again, and Marsha could hear it on her end of the call.

"What's going on?"

"I mean it, Marsha. This is an emergency. You've got to come help."

Craig took the steps down two by two. Tamara was in the dining room, toppling chairs and smashing vases. The last time he'd tried to subdue her during a tantrum he'd left marks on her arms. This time he just watched to make sure she wasn't going to hurt herself and tried to stay out of the way of flying objects.

The tornado migrated to the living room, where she knocked over a lamp, slung cushions onto the floor, and finally flung herself onto them and sobbed. Craig sat against the wall in the living room, watching his daughter, feeling helpless and guilty that he'd caused this tantrum to begin with.

Twenty minutes later, Marsha opened the front door to the chaos. She ignored Craig and went to her daughter, inspecting her from head to toe for injuries, then scooping her up and rocking back and forth. Tamara's tears and snot soaked Marsha's scrubs.

"What in the world?" She directed her anger at Craig.

"She blamed one of her *friends* again for her bad behavior. I only tried to reason with her." Craig was numb.

"Jefferson told me to, Mommy. He did."

"Jefferson?" Again directed at Craig.

"That thing right there, sitting on the windowsill. He started it. She's made a friend out of that black-and-white bird."

Marsha turned to the window.

"What bird?"

Craig stood and went to the pane. "Him, right here. The one that's not afraid to peer inside our home and drive our daughter stark raving mad."

Marsha lifted Tamara off her lap and joined Craig at the window. Marsha lowered her voice. "It's nice that you want to play along with her, but is that maybe what caused all this?"

"What do you mean, 'play along'?"

"There's nothing outside the window, Craig."

Tamara came to the glass. "Hi, Jefferson!"

The bird pecked at the window four times and lighted in the bush, watching the family. "That bird, Marsha, you don't see him? Don't you hear him pecking?"

"Mommy can't see him, Daddy. She can't see Samson, either." Tamara held open her hand, palm up, and a large, black ant stood on his back two legs, waving the middle and front pairs in mid-air.

"Tamara, put that down, that's nasty." Craig reached to rid her palm of the ant, but Tamara pulled her hand back.

Marsha got between her daughter and Craig. "Stop it," she whispered. "The more you feed into this nonsense, the harder it's going to be to get her help."

Craig looked around Marsha and Tamara, who was smiling and giggling. Now she held an ant *and* a spider. "Samson and Leo."

He rubbed his eyes and took a step away. He heard a buzzing near his ear, and a honey bee flitted near his head and he swatted at it.

"What's wrong with you?"

"Twila! Twila!" Tamara jumped up and down and the white-faced raven pecked the glass from outside again. "Don't swat at her Daddy, she won't sting."

"Marsha, please tell me you're seeing all this."

"Yeah, Craig, I see it. I see our daughter is a mess, the house is destroyed, and you're joining her in her delusions. I'm going back to work. Please clean this up and don't let her hurt herself." Marsha stormed out the door, leaving Craig, Tamara and the four imaginary friends to themselves.

"You *can* see them, all of them, right Daddy?"

Craig rubbed his eyes and buried his head in his hands.

"It's okay, Daddy. I was scared too at first. First you see them. Then you hear them. Then they're your friends."

When he looked up, all four critters and his daughter stared at him, waiting for some sort of reply.

But he had none. He'd joined his daughter in her delusion. He'd finally bonded with her and lost his mind in the process.

"Hey, look!" Craig followed Tamara's wild-eyed gaze out the window. There, under the oak tree, under the branch where Jefferson sat preening his feathers, waddled Craig's oldest friend. "Mr. Smithers says he's missed you!"

THE KEYS TO HAPPINESS

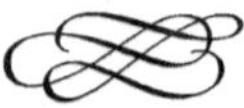

"What do you want most right this moment?"
It's a question the old man has asked hundreds of times — and will likely ask
hundreds more.
But will someone ever ask him what he desires most? Probably not in a
hundred lifetimes...

The old man stretched his legs in front of him and reached to run a tired hand through his chest-length beard. He gazed around at the sunny park. Not too busy. Not too empty. A perfect day to fulfill his never-ending duty.

He felt inside his left trouser pocket. He was almost out of supplies — and you'd think that would be a good thing. A good thing that twenty people today were happier than they were yesterday. A couple of them no doubt happier than they'd been in their whole life.

A runaway playground ball bumped into his feet. He raised one foot and rested his loafer on top of the bright blue orb. He straightened on the bench as a young boy, probably ten years old, gave chase.

"Thanks, Mister." The boy stooped for the ball, but the old man didn't move his foot. The boy looked straight into the wrinkled face. The old man knew the boy was mesmerized by the old man's crystal blue eyes; everyone was.

"No worries, son. No worries." He gave a grand smile to the lad and ran his hand through his beard once more.

The boy sat on the ground criss-cross style, still staring into the kind eyes. The old man removed his foot from the ball. The boy took it and put it in the middle of his lap.

"What can I help you with, son?"

"Are you Santa Claus? I mean. Well, I outgrew him. I mean—"

The old man laughed and shook his head. He often received this question from those under four feet tall. Sometimes even the adults would be daft enough to ask.

"I mean. I know how it works and all. I just… Are you him?"

"No. But I can help you." He pulled a silver chain from his left trouser pocket. One end of the chain remained deep inside the pocket. The other end held a ring of keys. Two days ago, the ring held forty-eight keys. He was down to twenty.

"Wow. What do all those keys open?" The boy broke gaze with the old man's eyes and was now mesmerized with the ring. "That one is awesome!"

The boys always like the skeleton keys. The grown men went for the car keys. The ladies the house keys. And the little girls could never decide. Stereotypical, but the old man never forced anyone to choose any certain key. It wasn't about the key's shape or the size, anyway. But they didn't know that.

"Would you like to have it?"

"Really? For keeps?"

"Almost for keeps." The man wriggled the ring around and around until the old skeleton key fell into his lap. He replaced the chain and ring into his left pocket and held the key for the boy to see, but just out of his reach.

"What do you mean almost?" The boy tipped his head to the side, his fingers fidgeted on top of his ball, and the old man knew the boy wanted to reach for it.

"Well, what do you want most right this moment?"

"I don't know." The boy still stared at the key.

"Well, think. If you could have any of your wants met right this moment, what would the most important one be?"

The boy brought a hand up to his chin and rested his elbow on the ball. His eyes lit up after a brief moment and he exclaimed, "Oh, I get it. It's like a wish. So you're like a genie or something."

"Or something." The old man smiled again and waved the key from side to side in front of the boy. He really needed to get on with this. He needed to restock today. The pawn stores and business offices would close around five o'clock. Last week, he found ten skeleton keys at the shops. The businesses in downtown had lost-and-found boxes under their desks. They never questioned or made the old, harmless man describe the keys he lost. Sometimes, they would return with several sets, and the man would choose the set with the most keys. After adding the batch to the chain in his left pocket, he would smile — like he smiled at the boy moments ago —and he would offer a key to the lady or gentleman who'd helped him recover his "lost set."

"But you must choose quickly." He told the lad. "Once the key is off the ring, its magic won't last forever."

The boy tapped on the ball again, clearly distressed about the deadline. "Well, I guess I'd like to wish for more wishes. But… that's probably against the rules, isn't it?"

The old man nodded. "You're a very keen child. Exactly one key. Exactly one wish. Exactly one minute left."

"Well, can I use it for someone else?"

"Absolutely." The old man's heart raced as the key vibrated in his hand. He sat up a little straighter on the bench. This had only happened once before, but the vibration faded when that young lady asked that her mother not die of cancer.

And the skeleton key stopped vibrating today once the boy spoke again.

"My baby sister, she's four. She's always wanted a cat, but we can't have any 'cause me and Dad are 'lergic. Can I give her a stuffed cat?"

Disappointed but not surprised, the man held out the key for the boy. He took it and turned it over in his hand. Usually, before anyone could ask "Now what?" the key worked its wonders. Slowly, slowly, it rose from the boy's open palm. In mid-air it twisted one-quarter turn, as if it were opening an invisible lock, then disappeared in a metallic sparkle.

Awe-struck, the boy's jaw dropped open. He looked at the old man, who gave one last smile, tucked his legs under himself to stand, and started to walk away.

"Oh man! Oh man! Thanks, Mister! It's even her favorite color."

He glanced behind him to catch sight of the boy running toward his family at the far end of the park. Plush purple cat tucked under his arm, blue ball bouncing off in the opposite direction.

Nineteen keys left.

THE OLD MAN removed his jacket and Oxford shirt and tossed them over the straight-back chair outside his bathroom door. He splashed water on his face, soaking his beard in the process. He glanced at himself in the mirror hanging from the green wall in the bathroom—which consumed about a tenth of the real estate in his studio apartment. He needed to move. He'd lived here for ten years now. A man his age would die soon. He needed a new place.

He retreated to the foot of his bed where he kicked off his loafers and unfastened the buttons on the left side of his trousers near the pocket that held the chain and keys. He slid the chain up and out, and let the pants fall to his ankles. He removed the ring of keys from the chain and placed them on his nightstand. The key-end of the chain snaked through a custom-made hole in the left side of his boxer shorts and dangled near his bare leg. He sat on the edge of the bed and put his head in his hands and sighed.

He managed to luck out with one lost-and-found at the corner of 20th and Park. He hadn't been there for about three years and thought he'd give it a try. He reached for his journal and made a note. He was always careful not to visit the same places too often. If he remembered clerks or secretaries, he would ask for the restroom and move on, keeping his eyes down.

He also made note of the little boy, his wish, the time of day and the location they met. Tomorrow he'd travel by subway two neighborhoods down to sit on the bench at the 10th Street bus stop.

He stood to crack open the window to let the cool spring air in. Locust trees from the street below gave off the sweetest aroma this time of year. He took a deep draw of the night air and drew the curtains to block the street lights.

He was weary.

He was weary fifteen decades ago.

He reached for the rubber band next to the key ring. He took the part of the chain that was near his thigh under his boxers and pulled it through the hole, freeing it over the waistband. He wound the length of it around his fingers over and over until he reached the end of the chain, which disappeared under his sixth rib. He attached the rubber band to secure it for the night and laid back in his bed.

He turned off the table lamp and draped his scrawny arm over his eyes. He remembered when an old man similar to himself had met him a few neighborhoods down when he was about the age of the boy with the blue ball.

He, too, had chosen a skeleton key.

"Well, what will it be, son?" the bearded one had asked of him.

"I like making people happy. I wish with all of my whole heart to make people happy forever and ever."

The man before him had wept, then apologized, and thanked him over and over. He hadn't understood the gentleman's reaction at the time.

But he did now.

The skeleton key had risen from his young hand, made a quarter-turn in mid-air, disappeared in a metallic wisp, and the chain appeared from under his rib, attached deep into his heart.

Forever and ever.

With his whole heart.

And the old man in front of him was relieved of his duties and had disappeared in the same metallic magic that took away the wished-upon keys.

He rolled to his right side to face the breeze and the sweet locust. He breathed deeply and felt the chain tug at his heart.

Tomorrow he would try again.

And maybe tomorrow, two neighborhoods down at the 10th Street bus stop, someone would finally hold the key to his happiness.

ATYPICAL MEDIUM

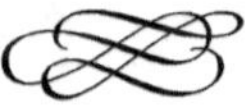

Declan's not your run-of-the-mill medium. Word down on afterlife avenue has it that Dec will only work with certain kinds of undead, and he keeps only a selective few on his payroll. And tonight, Declan's atypical team meets his parents...

THANKS to the standard American diet, the junk food offerings of Millburg Minimart consumed five of the seven aisles in the store. I gave a half-hearted effort to wipe the wet leaves from the bottoms of my boots on the worn entry mat, grabbed a lime green shopping basket with a tennis-ball-sized hole in the side, and headed toward all-things-cheese flavored.

Dad's favorites.

Mine, not so much. But tonight's reunion wasn't about me. Snacks for two. Or four. I glanced over my shoulder at Bev and Sol, unsure what the final headcount would be, so I erred on the side of plenty and headed for the checkout. Twice, the Cheezy Whippy can toppled through the basket's hole. I picked it up once. Solomon caught it midair the second time and returned it to the basket. I glared at him then around the shop. No one saw. Thank goodness.

The fall raindrops were still trickling from my scalp when I reached the register. I heard a couple of lady shoppers moan about the drop in temps and that the rainstorm has ripped nature's organic oranges and reds from the oaks. I'm glad for the change in weather. I used my free hand to zip my winter coat up to my Adam's apple, glad to no longer explain my choice of wardrobe or endure the curious stares when I choose to bundle up no matter the Fahrenheit level.

I sat the basket sideways on the counter for the clerk, a gaunt, tattooed young kid who couldn't make eye contact with me if his life depended on it. With each reach into the shopping basket, I watched the gooseflesh rise and multiply in ripples on the skin around his sweatshirt collar—despite the space heater's orange radiation stale warmth around us. Despite his long sleeves, double-layered shirts, and cut-out finger gloves. Despite the beanie on his head.

He was cold.

I know the look. The turtling of the head into the shoulders, chin to chest, eyes down. The bone-chilling freeze. Poor tortured soul. I'm accustomed to it by now, but by no means was one suffering from an ailment like mine ever comfortable.

Beverly and Solomon saw to that.

And the clerk could see my two ingrates. I nodded for them to leave the store ahead of me. Reluctantly, they did so, a trail of other-worldly gloom followed them out to the rain-soaked sidewalk. The kid dared a glance up.

Then right back down again.

I glance behind me, my eyes a little wider and a little more receptive than when I'd entered the store only a few minutes before—wide enough to see but not to take too much in. A skill learned over the years. Much like a baby playing peek-a-boo who truly believes he can't be seen behind a thin swaddle, I like to believe I can't be tagged if my lids hang at half-staff.

Three more lurked. One by the milk cooler. One by the stockroom door. One behind the chattering ladies in line behind me.

I wondered if these three follow the kid. I wondered if they've made their requests known. Or were they one of the hundreds of dead-but-no-so-dead ones that float and hover around those with the ailment. Begging. Haunting. Hanging on until we do their bidding.

Sometimes hanging around much past completion of their wishes.

I whip my head around toward my purchase, pay the kid in wadded-up bills from my pocket, and told him to keep the change. I didn't want any of them to know what I am.

What I can do.

I certainly didn't need this kid, God help him amid his curse, seeking counsel from me. I didn't need him to know what I am. That I'm like him in more ways than he'd imagine.

And I didn't need to add three more ghosts to my payroll.

Three is plenty, thank you very much.

I gathered the plastic sack of yellow and orange-powdered gut rot and joined my gang on the sidewalk. The rain had let up, but the drizzle tapped out an unkempt rhythm on the shopping bag. My boots swung through the mess of wet leaves, once kicking an empty soda can hidden underneath.

"No," I said to Sol.

He didn't listen and moved the can four feet down the sidewalk. Grinned at me, even. Taunting.

"Stop, Sol."

He couldn't resist cans and bottles. That's why he'd played with the cheese can in the store. Showing off. Letting off some pent-up ghoul. He'd been behaving rather well over the last few days. It was time for a show, I guess.

Solomon didn't listen and lifted the can five feet off the ground and sent it skimming through the rain like an air hockey puck, pinging off trees and stop sign poles until it was out of sight. He smiled and nodded at Beverly who rolled her eyes and huffed. She's never been a fan of Solomon's theatrics.

I wouldn't mind them, much like a toddler's mom can drown out ridiculousness as a matter of her own sanity. Keep the tot from touching the hot stove. Keep him from wandering into traffic. Maybe keep him from picking his nose, at least in public. But all the other stuff? Eat spaghetti with your toes. Fine. Repeat the last four words you heard the cartoon character say five hundred times. Fine. Wear a sock on one hand and Dad's underwear on your head. Fine. None of that stuff really matters.

Solomon's much like a toddler, but when he brings his antics to the street, Bev and I become more than a little miffed. His energy draws others. And, like I said before, I like to keep my payroll small.

I'm an atypical medium. I don't put up with the lonely and despaired, seeking to send great-grandmama a "love you, miss you, see you soon" message from beyond. I don't have time for that. And those poor souls, God rest their souls, have nothing to give me in return. They're time-sucks and soul-drainers.

And, unfortunately, many mediums fall victim to the ebbs and flows of the underworld, doing the bidding of a dozen undead at a time.

I'm not that kind. Not that kind of medium and not that *kind*. The pathetic kid at the checkout likely won't have a life past that checkout. Work, keep head down, send a few messages, repeat.

I could train him how to drown out all but the heavy hitters. How to profit off the past lives of criminals and colluders. And there really aren't that many of those type of ghosts around. The mobsters—I've served three. The serial killers—two of those so far, but the outcome wasn't pleasant, so I sent them on their way. The thieves—many. Solomon is my current employee and physical safe-cracker.

And there's Bev. She laundered the money for some pretty powerful people—all of them still living. And easily spooked, much to my wallet's joy. Her price was low and her return was high. She'd feed me account numbers if I kept her in touch with a few of her chosen ones still living. I've kept her on. And thank God the massive, large-breasted woman died with her bathrobe on. Tattered and blue with ripped pockets, her lighter always falling out. Hair pulled back in a messy gray bun. Cigarette still hanging out of her mouth, still releasing tendrils of smoky ribbons. Sometimes I swear I pick up a twinge of nicotine. She swears that's not how it works on her end. It's simply the power of suggestion.

Bev's voice is deep and gravelly, but she says that's not how it works, either. She wants me to go to an audiologist. So I can be proven wrong. So he can tell me all of my hammers, stapes, and anvils remain totally still as she rattles on about how she pulled one over on the governor. Or how the chief of police moved his mommy three counties over for fear that Bev—when she was on this side of the veil —would reveal to her his dirty scam. To prove me wrong once and for all that she telepaths her half of the conversation into my brain, bypassing the mechanics of my ears.

I, on the other hand, must speak my mind.

And carefully. A couple of times she'd gotten me so worked up in public that I yelled at her, drawing attention to myself from the living and dead alike. After that, she siphoned me an account number so I could afford a blue tooth. No one's the wiser if I have to correct one of my employees in public. Most people in the city have an earpiece of some sort while they walk sidewalks and hallways talking to them-selves. Now I do, too.

Solomon's thing is telekinesis. That's what I pay him for. I keep his great-grandchildren in school and educated and feed dollars into their mother's account when needed. He provides me with security. After all, I deal with death and dying, and my clientele are partial to all manner of weapons—the living and the dead.

We reach the corner where the pop can pinged its last. Solomon grinned, and I stepped on the can, smashing it flat and put it in the sack with the snacks. He stopped grinning. Bev wriggled her cigarette at me with her tongue and grinned. She likes it when Solomon pouts.

A couple more blocks in the damp before reaching home base. An apartment rental that Bev and Sol secured for me. A rare moment when the two worked seamlessly together, as they had a living contact in common. I supply Mrs. Fredrickson with news of her dead husband—one of Solomon's marks back in the day and, as it turns out, one of Bev's side-beaus. Mrs. Fredrickson loves to be angry, raging over his affairs (there were many) and his crimes (also multiple, and more coming to light as the months go on), so the intelligence my gang supplies, along with tidy sums of cash from an account Bev whispered into my brain (all Mr. Fredrickson's ill-gotten dough), keep me in well-appointed living quarters.

I fished my keys out of my pocket. Solomon could work the lock, but I didn't want him expending otherworldly energy out in the open, so I did it myself. The heavy steel gauge door swung into my space. Incense and potpourri of pumpkin spice and vanilla bean greet me. Any other would think it a warm, welcoming smell. I'm trying to mask Bev's smoke and Solomon's rot. Mrs. Fredrickson's never complained, and she's been down here many times. It's in my head if not my nostrils.

I sat the bag down on the counter and unpacked the snacks, lining them up just so. Cheese puffs. Balls. Curls. Chips. Crackers. Whippy. I glared at Solomon. "No. Leave the snacks." He slunk to the corner. I felt sorry for him, so I gave him the smashed can to mess with. He reflated it and clanged it off my chairs and table legs. Like handing a toddler a wooden spoon and a pot lid. Bev rolled her eyes and hefted herself to the corner. Man, I'm always so glad she died with her clothes on.

I took off my soaked jacket and scarf and hung them on the backs of the table chairs to dry. I turned up the thermostat. Always set on seventy-six, I cranked it to eighty-two. I knew it wouldn't help, but it made me feel better.

He'd be here shortly. For our yearly ritual of snacking and VHS reruns. My dad. And he'd likely bring in the cold.

I sat back in my recliner. I'd sprung for the heated one with massage capabilities. I figured I deserved it after all I put up with. Bev wished she could sink her tired essence into a recliner. I waved her off. I wasn't in the mood to listen to her whine. Solomon, tired of the can, retreated to his corner opposite Bev. They watched me as I examined the sheet I'd hung before our outing to procure the snacks. A white bedsheet draped from a fishing line that I'd secured in hooks on the wall. A projector, old school, so Solomon had worked it through Bev who worked the setup into my head so I could go big screen this year.

Because I'd planned on not doing this again. To go out big and be done with this ritual.

How much longer can it go on? I dreaded telling Dad, but he needed to move on.

I'm getting nothing but grief for my trouble. Exactly what I try to avoid at all costs. Grief and grieving.

I work tit for tat. I won't be horrified or tormented into helping those masses, no matter how many of them try to find me. Most have given up thanks to an informant I once served. I delivered four messages for Gregory and then charged him to do what he did best when he was on this side of the sidewalk. Inform. Inform as many of the between-worlds kind that Declan Morose isn't for hire. Declan Morose is an atypical medium and they should find some other sensitive spirit to taunt and tickle.

Gregory had done his job well. Between his word out on the street and a dozen tricks I'd learned over forty years on the job, I'd whittled the chaos down to two main buddies and the occasional side job.

Gregory had tried to give the message to my dad. But Pop would have none of it and had insisted from his deathbed night until now that we stay in touch.

Once a year. For the last fifteen years.

Same lineup of cheesy snacks.

Same movie.

The gooseflesh prickled down my spine. The furnace struggled to keep the thermostat's needle in the sixties.

He'd arrived. I glanced toward the kitchen, following Solomon's hollow eyes and Bev's slightly startled gawk.

Great. Dad brought Mom.

I studied them and sighed.

The kind of ghouls I served weren't that needy in real life. Hardcore criminals rarely fall into that category. And most of them were only slightly needy in their deaths.

Dad, though. I should be glad he visits just once a year. He thought late October would do fine, seeing as how I'd be incredibly busy after the first of the year. Most unlearned think that Halloween and the thirteenths that fall on Fridays are busy times for mediums. January and February are the worst. Post-holiday let-downs and February's lost loves have a way of sucking souls from bodies. I tend to stay indoors and do extra bidding for Sol and Bev. So they can be my bouncers.

I stood and faced the kitchen. Faced my parents. Dead. Dad fifteen years. Mom five. No amount of bouncing nor informing nor tits-for-tats could keep my parents away from me this year.

"What's up?"

Mom shrugged, guilt trip pouring off her see-through shoulders.

Dad rolled his eyes. "Can we be a family this year? Just once?" He flicked a bony hand toward the sheet where Bev and Sol hovered.

"No. They stay."

"I have something to tell you, Dec. I don't want an audience."

"I always have an audience, Dad. You know this." I'd asked Bev a few years ago if I was hearing my father speak to me or if he was planting thoughts like she did. She rolled her eyes. Told me he wasn't that talented of a ghost and probably never would be. He was speaking. I was hearing. It was simple.

I unscrewed the lid from the Cheezy Whippy and opened the crackers. "Want some?" I offered a loaded saltine to my mother. She loathed junk food. Never let me eat anything after school but grapes and apples. Even blamed my ailment on the sugar content of the elementary school's chocolate milk. Dad had tried to explain it to her. She'd have none of it. I think she's come around now, though.

"Not funny, Declan." She turned her back to me. Her blouse billowed around her waist. I couldn't see what color. I knew she was in jeans and a teal shirt when she passed. But I couldn't make out the color. Bev had been with me for such a long time that I could pick details out on her form that I couldn't on the fresh ones. Mom, much to my dismay, was considered a fresh one. Destined to hover for quite some time. "Not funny at all. And I don't appreciate that insensitive Gregory fellow telling me to stay away from my only son."

I stuffed the cracker in my mouth, the salt sucking away what little moisture was there. I wanted a water bottle from the fridge, but I wasn't going to step into the kitchen. With my parents. No matter how thirsty I was. I wasn't sorry Gregory warned Mom off. She could bother someone else with her woe.

I turned back to the projector setup. I popped in the VHS tape and adjusted the volume as the images began to dance on the screen in front of us.

"Wait a minute, Dec. We need to talk." The pause button depressed on the VCR. I glared at Solomon. He floated backward with palms up. Wasn't him. He always took gloating credit for his tricks.

I pressed play again.

Pause depressed.

Mother. That's why he'd brought her. Dad couldn't telekenese and he wanted my attention.

"No. We need to watch this, so you and Mom can be appeased and on your way."

"I taught you better, Dec. I taught you to listen with your gift. To help people. Not to simply appease." The 's' on appease slithered out of him snake-like. A scare tactic. Overused and underrated.

"Not a gift, Dad." I pressed play down and held it there. Solomon grinned. He wasn't the only one I'd had to bully into behaving today. "An ailment."

Dad glared at Mom who fumed and popped open the bag of cheese puffs, sending a spray of crumbs and orange dye all over the kitchen floor.

"Blasphemy."

"Tell that to the poor kid at Millburg Mart. Or the ones that walk hunched over in the mall trying to buy underwear in peace, bombarded by broken souls. Try telling that to me, Dad. At the ripe old age of three when you found out I could talk to the dead, you *used* me."

The scene escalated quickly. We'd never talked like this before. Always a playful ritual around the snack counter. Always a sit-down-and-watch moment, and then he'd leave.

"I *developed* you." He slid forward, nose to nose with me, only the thin veil between life and death separating his exhales from my inhales. Bev moved behind me, ready for action, her nicotine, usually revolting, now comforting and strong in my senses. Solomon hovered near Mom, ready for ghost-on-ghost defense.

I pressed play again. Not to be bullied or horrified. Dad allowed it, calling Mom off. The gears in the VCR spun the images of childhood one after the other. My coming-home day. My various birthdays. Learning to ride a bike.

The home movie attempted to mark milestones of normalcy. Dad and I had watched this film for years. I'd often wondered what would happen when the tape wore out. I don't have a backup. I'm not nostalgic. Why would I be? The images in front of me are from one tiny pocket of my childhood. The other pockets were stuffed to overflowing with ghosts and devils and Dad gaining from it. I never understood why he wouldn't move on. I'd figured it was out of guilt for using me.

As if sensing what I was thinking, he said, "This is what I wanted to talk to you about." He nodded toward Mom.

"I need to come clean." He leaned in close and whispered to me, "So *she* can move on. I'm tired of her neediness. Of being shunned by so many here because she's got such a temper. Gregory did a number on the other mediums. They won't take my calls."

"You've got to be kidding me."

"I figure if I come clean about what I did," he nodded toward Mom, "She can be at peace."

"What you did was bleed your son of any real life instead of getting him the help he needed." Mom winced when I said this. She'd not believed me or dad. Thought us to be playing games. An inside father-and-son joke.

Dad looked confused. Through his form I could see the kitchen behind him and the mess Mom had made. She continued to flick cheese curls onto the floor. "What? I'm not sorry for how I raised *you*. I'm sorry for what I did to *her*." He pointed to Mother.

"What are you talking about?" She asked.

He moved toward her. On this side, he'd have put an arm around her shoulders and lead her to the couch to have a chat. On that side, all he could do was hover. She pulled back.

"What are you talking about?"

"Miriam. Sweetheart. I'm the reason you died."

Her eyes widened. My eyes widened. Solomon and Bev withdrew closer to the curtain where ten-year-old Declan took a forward-flip into the neighbor's swimming pool. The tape failed to pick up the three bodies floating in the pool. Souls of bodies, anyway. I'd always been terrified of that pool. When a kid tells you they don't want to jump off the diving board, there may be more than one reason why.

The temperature dropped another five degrees. My poor furnace. "What do you mean, Dad? Mom had a heart attack."

He straightened his form and hovered over the recliner. "That's what they thought it was. But I did it. I needed some company. I was lonely, Dec. You ostracized me. You and that Gregory fellow. But now I just need her to move on. It's not the same as it used to be—"

A shrill shriek like that from a school bus about to lose its brakes escaped from the depths of my mother. The VCR ground to a halt, pausing twelve-year-old me in flannel Christmas pajamas on the fluttering bedsheet before disappearing in an explosion of sparks and plastic bits. Solomon froze a few of the pieces just inches from my face. Gears and black ribbon from the crushed VHS drifted to the floor when he released his hold.

Bev told me to duck. I did so, barely clearing my scalp of the flying jar of cheese balls. It exploded with a pop against the walls. Balls in the living room. Curls in the kitchen. Mom wreaking havoc with the Cheezy Whippy can while Dad tried to calm her.

Solomon was in his element. Catching and flinging containers, curls, and balls back at hollow forms that would never feel the impact —but my walls could. I told him to stop throwing, just catch. I hoped Mrs. Fredrickson had her hearing aids turned down.

"Duck again," Bev said. She'd nestled herself in the corner, grinning with that dumb cigarette that never burned out hanging from her mouth. I listened and turned in time to see a spray of orange goo heading toward my head, the slime splattered all over the sheet in bright drips. Thank God it missed the recliner.

"How long you gonna let this go on?" Bev asked.

"How long you gonna float there until you earn your keep?" I snarked back.

Bev laughed and hovered horizontally over my enraged mother, her hands reaching down toward Mom's head. I couldn't hear what she said. But then again, Bev wasn't *saying* anything. Mom looked up at Bev, gave her two middle fingers and then tunneled through the wall to the outside, leaving a trail of orange powder, goo, and crumbs smudged on the paint job in her wake.

Dad's form froze, staring at me.

"That went well, I think." I fished the broom from the side of the fridge and began cleaning up the remnants of the temper tantrum. Solomon tried to help, but toddler that he is, created more work as he played with the cheese balls and exploded the occasional puff in putrid orange dust balls.

Dad still said nothing. "Movie's over, Dad. Destroyed like my childhood. You can move on. Mom certainly isn't ready, not with the issues she needs to work through."

This enraged him. His plan had backfired. He wanted to be free in the in-between. Now Mom was loose, and his time was up. He tried to say something, but the process had already begun. He'd cleared his conscience. The veil was clearing him out, pulling him to a place beyond the reach of any earthly medium.

I didn't feel anything. No pity. No sorrow. My ailment had caused our family so much dysfunction. One parent exploited me. One parent ignored my pain. And given what I've seen over the years, I'm not easily surprised. Not even that Dad had drug Mom to the in-between.

I continued to sweep up the cheese dust from the hardwood floors. Solomon played with the black VHS ribbon, ignoring his empty cans and containers. He'd found a new toy for the moment. I put the broom down to empty my wax pot. There were cheese curls in my pumpkin vanilla spice. I'd rather smell Bev's smoke.

A knock on the door stalled my cleaning. I hoped it wasn't Mrs. Fredrickson coming to see what the chaos was about. I opened the door a crack, then let a fall gust blow it all the way open.

The kid from the minimart stood in front of me. Bundled tight in layer upon layer. His head ducked at first, then slowly rose to meet me. He took in the scene behind me. I followed his gaze. Cheese everywhere. Cheesy floors. Cheesy sheet flapping in the wind against the wall. His pale face flashed red then back to ghost white again as he saw the VHS tape dance in a hollow mummy form, Solomon's puppet on a black ribbon string. Bev hovered in the kitchen like an old bat looking for a place to land, dropping unreal ashes onto the piles of really real cheese curls.

I looked back to the kid who met my gaze full on.

"Sir. Would you please do something about your mother?"

Bev stopped her hovering. Solomon dropped the ribbon into a piled heap on the floor.

"You've got to help him, Dec," Bev said.

"I know." The kid thought I was talking to him. Bev knew I was responding to her. I looked behind him. In the midafternoon drizzle, a growing line of pathetics waited their turns to speak with this poor tortured soul. "Bev, call Gregory." This would mean more work for me. More time out in public. I'd owe all three ghouls on the payroll, but I couldn't turn my back on the kid.

"You want to come in?"

He stood frozen at the doorway. Shivering.

"Listen, kid. You can come inside with me and this mess and these two freaks, or you could stay out here with your paparazzi—"

He nearly knocked me over. Bev stood guard until Gregory showed lest the three forms from the minimart—and my mother—should try to enter. I offered to take the kid's coat, but he clutched to his layers. "Got anything left to eat?"

"Got a name?"

"Aaron."

I tossed him a sleeve of saltines that had escaped my mother's rage. "Well, Aaron, the cheese on the sheet should still be edible."

He shrugged and swiped a cracker across the homemade movie screen. Delivering messages for the dead or eating sprayed-out condiments from a bedsheet—it's all in a day's work.

I watched Aaron as he watched Solomon, who'd returned to molding monster shapes with the VHS tape. The kid quit shivering the more crackers he ate. A few hours before, I'd been willing to leave him to his demise. The price all mediums pay. But my mother was contributing to his misery and no one deserves that.

I thought of the payouts I'd have to split. The ghostly employees we'd have to share. Lots of learning to take place over the next few months. Years, actually. It'd taken me a good decade to put together my posse, and some of those decided to go the way of Dad and move on.

But Aaron wouldn't have to spend his days in misery at Millburg's earning minimum wage one hour, doing the dead's dirty work the next.

He'd spend them here with me. Out of the ebb and flow of the underworld. Learning not to be so scared. Not to be a target of the dead's beckoning. Learning to grow a backbone.

Learning to be a bit…atypical.

THE KILLING JAR

When twins Jessica and James are assigned a school project to capture and mount a slew of insects, they clash over his enthusiasm and her apathy— until things get out of hand one night and the butterfly whispers she imagined as a child turn out to be not so imaginary.

The kids pushed their way off the bus and through the front door. Jessica dragged her backpack to the kitchen, where she was only slightly uplifted by the aroma of something baking. Something with brown sugar…

James was elated and had been since fourth period. He didn't need sweets to improve his mood.

"What's up with you guys? Looks like you two attended school in different universes today." Their mother had cleaned the kitchen, though Jessica wasn't sure why—it'd be a mess in a few minutes after James raided the fridge and cleaned out the cabinets. He never stopped eating.

"Mrs. Krebbs's class is doing that entomology project. We have to gather ten species and attach them to this." James spilled the contents of his backpack onto the counter.

"I never wanted to sign up for this dumb class." Jessica gingerly pulled out a ten-by-ten-inch piece of foam core board and set a tube of pins next to it. "It was this or the dissection class for graduation. I hate this."

"Here, have a cookie before James eats them all." Mom pushed a plate of chocolate goodness toward Jessica's nose.

"Cookies don't solve everything, Mom."

"Well, they sure don't hurt anything." Mom crammed half of one into her mouth. "Besides, how do you think you'll get through medical school if you can't handle a simple insect collection?"

Jessica slumped across the counter. Perhaps there was a different way to save people without having to cut things up. Maybe social work…

James reached over and grabbed four cookies and headed upstairs. Jessica's twin, older by five minutes, James couldn't wait to capture bugs and push the fasteners into their body parts, legs going every which way. On the bus, he'd shown her a checklist of the insects he hoped to capture. He was sure to get an A.

Jessica didn't mind the work, but had asked whether she could please print out photos from Google and research that way. Or sketch them. Mrs. Krebbs had said no. Jessica had taken the mounting supplies from her teacher, but she'd refused the butterfly net; they already owned a couple.

Jessica took half a cookie and went to the garage to rummage in the corners for the nets she knew they hadn't thrown away. If spiders were insects, she could've had the project done and over with already, as several greeted her from the dark corner of the garage. Her skin crawled and she brushed them away, resisting the urge to stomp them flat.

Behind hockey sticks that hadn't been used past one season and squatty T-ball bats she didn't know why they kept, she found the two nets the kids had begged their parents for years ago. She pulled on them, and rakes and forgotten golf clubs came clamoring down.

She left the mess and let the pink material of the butterfly netting run through her fingers. The blue one was in bad shape, with a giant hole in the main part of the net—the hole she'd put in it that day with the apples.

Seven years ago, the twins had pitched the four-person tent in the back yard after Dad got called away for business for the weekend and couldn't take them camping. He was always away on business, it seemed.

The neighbor's apple tree grew unruly and a branch drooped over their privacy fence, dropping the sourest apples on the planet into their yard. Dad complained, but the neighbors didn't care. He'd threatened to cut the branch away from their fence, but never got around to it.

The inedible apples attracted all manner of wasps, bees and the biggest butterflies imaginable. Monarchs, swallowtails and buckeyes with the giant black spots on their brown wings.

James complained about the lumpy apples under the tent floor, and a couple of the bees tried to get into the tent, but the kids shooed them out. Then a butterfly, a purple emperor, came in with Jessica on her shoulder. It stayed there for quite some time, pumping its beautiful scaled wings. Jessica thought she could hear it whisper to her before lighting on her camp roll.

"I have an idea!" Jessica stepped outside the tent, found an apple with a brown swallowtail enjoying its nectar, and carefully carried the insect into the tent. James did the same with a small, dusty yellow sulfur. They'd close the tent's mesh screen behind them each time. Their fingers stuck to one another—and to the tent's zipper—from the juice of the rotten apples, but soon they had ten butterflies inside the tent.

It was at this point that they decided—Jessica couldn't remember whether it was her idea or James's—that nets would be much easier. Since the kids were engaged and outside instead of inside muddying up the place, their mom agreed to run out and purchase the nets. Pink for Jessica. Blue for James. An entire morning and afternoon of fun for about ten bucks.

Their mother soaked paper towels with sugar water and wrung them out. She placed them on plates inside the tent. Before long, the butterflies found their way to the sweet treat and spent considerable time drinking from the towels, opening and closing their wings in silent contentment.

By the afternoon, the tent held dozens and dozens of butterflies. Jessica sat in the middle of the tent on her bed roll. When James wasn't running his mouth, she could hear their wings flutter along the edges of the tent. She closed her eyes and imagined they whispered secrets to her. Secrets only she could be trusted with.

She imagined so hard that some of the whispers felt real, breaths of softness near her ear. Whispers of thanks. Whispers of adventure.

Several landed on her knees and shoulders. One plain brown one landed on her hand. She brought it close to her face and could see its mouth parts working along her skin.

Then James discovered something. If you ran your fingers along the butterflies' wings, the color came off in glittery dust, leaving an almost see-through spot on the wing. Jessica caught him stripping the scales from the purple emperor. He'd captured it in his blue net and had it trapped against the mesh, his fingers a mess of black and purple. "Look, sis!"

"Stop it!" Jessica reached for the net, ripped a hole in it and allowed the butterfly to escape.

James got mad and tried to catch another one from inside the tent.

"No!" Jessica undid the zipper to the tent and opened the two small window zippers inside. She shooed and shooed until only a couple of stubborn ones on the sugar water towels remained.

"Why'd you let them go?" James had complained. To her, to Mom, and to Dad the next week. Everyone told him to get over it. Jessica had felt vindicated, but she'd never forget the damaged wings, nor the few butterflies that lay at the bottom of the tent, the ones that had used up their lifespan that very day, or maybe were injured during transport, never to flutter again.

Jessica went into the house with the pink net. James was at the counter with one of Mom's half-gallon Mason jars, the great big one she and Grandmother used to make homemade apple cider in. The one with the small crack starting at the mouth of the glass.

"What are you doing?"

"Oh, cool. You found the net. That'll help." He screwed the lid onto the jar. Two wet cotton balls sat in the base. "The internet had complicated instructions for kill jars, but I just used mom's fingernail polish remover. We'll put the bugs in, and they'll die. I wanted to freeze them, but Mom said no."

"That's right," Mom said from behind them. "Everything out to the porch. Now. No dead bugs in here at all."

"Not even to mount them?" James asked.

Jessica's stomach began to knot up.

"No, out on the porch. Now."

"But it's for Mrs. Krebbs—"

"I don't much care if it's for Mrs. Krebbs or for the Pope. Outside." Mom escorted the twins from the kitchen.

THE FAMILY'S home sat on a corner lot. Behind the lot was a long stretch of road and field. A deep ditch ran along both sides of the road. Some areas of the ditch held water, and cattails and pussy willows had decided to make it home. James thought the tall, grassy culvert would be a good place to start looking.

Jessica carried the net. James carried the jar. "I figure if we can each get five or six today, that's half the project. But I want something different. Something big for the center of the board."

Mrs. Krebbs offered extra credit for anyone in the class who had a species that no one else had. So, if everyone had a green grasshopper, good for them. But if only one person found a walking stick or a praying mantis, they'd get extra credit. James was a suck-up when it came to grades and would do anything to impress the teachers.

Jessica was a good student, but extra credit for rare species turned her off.

James hopped into the ditch, away from the marshy area. As he did, dozens of grasshoppers flew and jumped in all directions.

"The net, the net!"

Jessica came to herself and swooped the net over the top of the grass tips, capturing four hoppers for the trouble. James opened the jar, and the stringent acetone made Jessica's eyes water.

"Dump them in here."

"They're all the same. We only need two."

"Yeah, but we can decide which ones are best later. One may have a broken leg or something."

"We only need two." Jessica worked their spiked legs loose from the netting and plopped two into the jar. She turned the net inside out and let the others go.

"You're gonna be a pain all through this, aren't you?" He screwed the lid onto the jar as Jessica gave him a light crack across the butt with the net. The grasshoppers evaded the cotton balls, clinging to the top of the jar. James tried to shake them down, but their instinct to live was too great. Jessica's stomach turned again, but she was ready to gather the specimens and get this part over with.

By the time Mom texted that dinner was ready, they had grasshoppers, crickets, a couple of dull brown moths and two different kinds of beetles. They left the bugs and net on the covered porch and went in for the meal. James didn't stop talking about myriads of mounting techniques and what they might find at the ditch in the morning.

Then Dad piped up and showed James a picture on his phone.

When he showed Jessica, she stormed off without finishing her meal.

⁓

"IF YOU DON'T HELP, I'll tell Mrs. Krebbs that I did all the work for your project."

"Of course you will, because you're a jerk." Jessica pulled the rope tight around the maple tree, yanking the other end of the rope from James's hand. He shot her a glare and tied his end to the clothesline post left over from the previous owners. Mom never used it and wanted it gone—another project that Dad was going to do and never got done; he even complained that he had to mow around it every week, like the old cobblestones that dotted the back yard. Jessica and James used to play hopscotch over them, but now they'd sunk into the grass enough to make mowing a bumpy ordeal.

After the pair tied off the rope, they threw two white twin sheets over the line. Dad helped them rig up utility lights to shine directly on the sheet. The idea he'd found was to attract moths and nighttime bugs. The insects couldn't resist the light, and would land on the sheet, making them easier to snatch up in the net.

As dusk fell, James turned on the utility lights and the siblings sat on the back porch, waiting and watching.

James scrolled through dozens of websites on his phone for ideas on mounting, labeling and presentations. Jessica pouted, trying not to cry. She picked up the Mason jar and removed the lid. The grasshoppers had died with their eyes open. She didn't know if they had eyelids or not, though.

She dumped them all out of the jar and took out the cotton balls, still reeking of fingernail polish remover.

"Hey, those probably need to be re-soaked." James went in and was back in a moment with Mom's bottle of acetone. He re-wet the cotton and stuck it back in the jar. They divvied up the bugs. James took the biggest and brightest. Jessica didn't care.

A *pop, pop, popping* on the screen door got their attention. June bugs, the beetles with amber-colored armor, hit the side of the house, then buzzed away toward the sheet.

"If we turn the porch light off, they'll concentrate on the sheet." James flicked off the light and they sat in darkness, watching the bugs hit the white screen and fly off into the night. A few of them stayed, but the beetles proved easy to catch. James was waiting for something magnificent. They sat in silence for a while.

Then Jessica heard a whisper over her right shoulder. She couldn't make it out and dismissed it as stress and replaying the memories of the tent.

Then it happened again.

She went to the screened window on the right side of the porch. The halogen bulbs aimed at the sheet gave barely enough light to make out the arrival. A moth, at least a whole hand-span wide, clung with all six legs to the holes in the screen. Its body was thick, and through the shadowed light she could make out the furriness of its head.

And then the whisper again.

Save us.

Fear. It had to be fear that James would find the creature and cram it into the jar. She turned quickly to face him, hiding the moth behind her shoulders, hoping the thing would stay put and not succumb to the lure of the bright light around the corner.

"What is it?" James could read her well. The twin thing was getting old.

"Nothing. Needed to stretch."

"Liar." He shoved her aside. As he did, the moth took off, directly into the light.

"That's mine! I call it." He ran outside with the net, unscrewing the lid to the killing jar as he went.

"You don't need it. Not that one. Leave it be," Jessica pleaded as

James set down the jar on one of the sunken cobblestone stepping stones and shoved the lid into his back pocket.

"This is the extra credit one, I know it." He raised the net, ready to swoop down on the green and purple Luna moth hanging near the top of the sheet.

Jessica grabbed his arm. "You already have an A in Mrs. Krebbs's class. You don't need this one."

"You dummy. It's gonna die soon anyway. What is it, like a five- or six-day life span? I may as well have it." He shrugged Jessica off and raised the net again.

"No! It won't even fit in the dumb jar." She yanked hard on his arm. The motion startled the moth, which took off, its tapered wings fluttering, swooping up to the stars, then back down toward the light, its body like the glow-in-the-dark stick-on stars on her ceiling. On its downward path, James leapt with the net, barely missing twice.

"No!" As the Luna took one more swoop toward the sheet, Jessica lunged at her brother, knocking him off balance and sending him crashing to the ground. The pink net landed somewhere beyond his head. Jessica landed on top of him with all her weight.

James cried out and looked at Jessica stunned, like the wind was knocked out of him.

"Get up." She rolled off him. "Stop being a baby."

But James didn't move. She nudged his ribs with her foot and he winced, but just barely.

"Are you really hurt, or are you yanking my chain?" She knelt beside him. Her heart started to beat in her ears and sweat formed on her lip. "James?"

He reached up with his right arm, elbow stationary at his side. She pulled on his hand, and he met the tug with a wail of pain.

"Mom, Dad!" Jessica screamed and tried to set James upright, but he shook his head and she left him in the grass. She called again for her parents, already at her side. The three of them lifted James into a sitting position, and he wailed again.

On his back, shards of the Mason jar glistened in the halogen work lamps. Glass stuck out from his shirt, blood pooling around the edges. Another pool of blood soaked the cobblestone.

Jessica lost track of time and sensation. She sat with her left leg propping James up from behind, careful not to touch the wounds. He slumped into her chest, her right leg draped across his lap while her parents rushed to do she knew not what.

"I'm so sorry. James, I'm so sorry. I never meant—"

He gasped but couldn't speak. He raised his arm up and brushed her cheek with his fingertips, then dropped his hand into her lap.

She could hear commotion but didn't process what was said to her. Numbness closed in, tunneling her away from reality.

Paramedics.

She felt someone unwrapping her from her brother. Untangling them. Lifting him away. Leaving her alone.

The sound of metal on metal. A stretcher being raised to position, maybe.

She sat in the damp grass, knees pulled up to her chest and stared at the sheet. Blue and red lights chased each other across the white screen.

A wail from her mom. Then her dad.

Then a whisper.

The Luna moth flitted in front of her face, hovered, then landed on her knee.

Jessica didn't move. She didn't breathe. The grieving world fell away bit by bit as the creature folded its wings to the resting position. Its body, covered with a fur-like pelt, quivered gently.

Another whisper. This time louder.

Jessica inhaled slowly. Slowly disassociated from the chaos and cries around her.

She brought her head down to meet the creature's black gaze, it's yellow-ferned antennae moved side to side, feeling the air.

A silver harness, no thicker than a spider's silk, shimmered around the moth's head. She unbent her knee slightly and traced the silver thread to the creature's back.

The Luna moth's miniature rider, bathed in the same colors as the moth itself, sat atop a perfectly camouflaged green saddle. Her wings opened and closed in time with the flashes of blue and red dancing behind her. The tiny woman hung her head for a moment when Jessica made eye contact. When she lifted it, a purple tear trickled down her cheek.

She offered a sorrowful whisper before she tugged the harness and spurred the Luna to take flight, *"Thank you."*

MALACHI MAXWELL

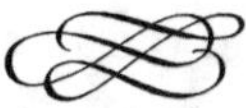

A Mag-Line Mini Mystery

*Renee, a through-and-through dog person, finds herself caring for not one,
but three feline rescues. Her latest little fur baby, Malachi Maxwell, gives her
a run for her money with health issues, toe troubles and maybe just a hint of
magical chaos to keep things interesting...*

I'm sitting here at the vet's office—a place all-too-familiar when you're a more-than-middle-aged animal lover in a small town. There's only one place to go. Doc Whitby's, with its always-full gravel lot—watch your step, not all of those round bits are gravel. Glass entry doors with slobber and sneeze snot spots. High-backed Formica benches replaced the old burgundy vinyl seating that had sported nail punctures and the smell of sick. A shelf of high-end nutritional options for canines and felines spans one wall.

A frequent flyer here, I've used the free-standing clean-up station with the toweling dispenser and antiseptic cleanser more than once. The waiting room always smells of wet dog and antiseptic, even when you're the first patient on the roster. Windows out to the highway span the other wall, letting in the faintest of early morning June rays. It's cloudy—gray clouds at that. That gravel lot will be muddy soon enough. When Spencer was with us, I would've worried about the potential for thunderstorms. Thunder freaked that pooch out bigtime. But no need to worry about that today. I'm here with Malachi and the fur ladies back home don't worry about storms—they're much too dignified for that.

Tammy, Dr. Whitby's older-than-time tech, and Zara, the fresh new girl, scurry at the computers tucked behind the check-in counter. Today's scrub color is aqua. Because it's Tuesday. Yesterday would have been burgundy and tomorrow the techs will wear navy. I told you I'm a first-name basis frequent flyer here.

"Be with you and Malachi in a moment, Renee." Tammy whizzes back and forth shuffling charts and lines of prescriptions waiting to be picked up. "It's gonna be crazy today."

"No worries," I say. When is it not crazy at Doc Whitby's?

Around the rim of the counter, a few metal hooks protrude to secure leashes while the credit cards come out and discharge paperwork is completed. Short girl problems, I've had my fair share of bruised arms from those hooks on the elevated counter, wrestling dogs of old and cats of current...

And then there's the battery-operated flameless pillar candle. With the cute/comforting poem that's neither cute nor comforting. If the candle is lit, it means someone's in the goodbye-for-now room and lets those waiting their turn know to keep the chaos to a contained minimum. I know. I've been in that room many times with many fur babies over the years.

The candle's not lit this morning. I'm glad for that.

And don't worry. My tale doesn't end with a glow from that candle. Just so you can relax. Keep the Kleenex for another time.

The most interesting thing in the whole waiting room is the much-dreaded and completely terrifying three-inch-high weighing platform. I swear they should set up a camera aimed solely at that scale. Make a fortune on viral videos of dogs doing the freak-out-four-step when the owners and vet techs try to coax the poochy patients onto the stainless-steel demon.

I look at the hard-sided carrier next to me and bend to peek at Malachi through the door. He blinks at me with those gorgeous lazy eyes of his, never fully opened. Always looking like he's just waking up, even at his most alert. "Keep your socks on, buddy." I wave a finger at him through the grate. He blinks again.

My handsome man. White and tabby. Mostly white. Black beans and pink beans and some half black and half pink. Oh, those beans are why we're here... I think.

We'd named him Maybelline when we'd thought he was a she. I'm a dog person. I had no idea how to sex a cat, let alone a malnourished fragile bit of fur. But those eyes, outlined in thick black and blended up into the stripes on the sides of his face looked like he'd just exited the makeup artist's chair. When we realized he was a he and not a she, we adjusted the name. Malachi Maxwell.

And so you know, all of our critters have had middle names—or two or three middles sometimes—and several nicknames. That's just part of being a family.

There was Blossoms Beverly the Boston Terrier. There was Bandit Bulldog, also a Boston. Boomer—I was too little to remember his middle, but I know there was one. Chloe Patches—motherly mutt of a cocker/lab mix. Spencer Doodles—a high maintenance seizure-prone

Schnauzer. Winston Walter Conrad—English bulldog with such high-end medical issues we nearly pitched a tent outside in the poopy gravel.

My next dog will be a Dane. Large, lanky. Female. Preferably brindle or tawny, but any color will do. Already have a name string picked.

Neema Suellen Grace. See? I'm a dog person.

There was that first cat, though. Cosmo Quasimodo. Made it sixteen years. Never intended to have a cat—ever. But when you're walking with your four-year-old and she tells you that God himself sent her this flea-bitten mangy cat and the child starts dancing in the street, singing praises to the Almighty... Well, who was I or her father to tell her that Cosmo wasn't the cat God had picked out for her. That critter made his home in ours for sixteen years. But he was raised by Chloe Patches and Spencer Doodles, so he never really was very cat-ish. I think having dog parents broke part of his feline instincts.

I peek into the carrier again. Malachi's chilled, stretching in his blue plastic hideout like he's done this a thousand times. He hasn't, he's not a year old yet. And, unfortunately, he's not a dog, so I won't get the pleasure of a performance at the scales. The tech will take him and the carrier to the back and weigh them in private. Like cats care what the outcome will be.

I'm a dog person.

How I ended up with three cats is beyond me.

The door chime signals an incoming wave of guaranteed chaos. I scoot on the bench a little further down and away from the glass door. I can already hear toenails scratching the tile floor and an owner barking ignored instructions. "Calm down. Calm down."

I brace my hand over Malachi's crate. He's still chilled. Nothing bothers him. Nothing. The dog—a black and white Dane!—comes pulling her owner through the waiting area, legs going everywhere. Drool flying. The lady, a petite twenty-something, is no match for the dog's energy. Tammy springs to action.

"Why don't you go ahead and put Gypsy on the scales and we'll take her back. We've got some more cats coming—"

Gypsy puts her front feet onto the counter, knocking over the candle and sending the plastic-framed poem to the floor.

Zara, who'd went to prep a room, came running from the hall to assist, her black ponytail coming undone as she helped wrestle the dog. Everyone's yelling and grabbing, and I'm not fast enough with my camera to shoot footage of the fiasco at the scales. I'm telling you, there's money to be made there.

The owner ends up on her butt, looking up at Gypsy and trying to reason with the pooch that if she'd just stand still she'd get a treat. The dog's hindquarters vibrate with fear and nervous energy and Zara finally gives the all-clear. They'd gotten the weight—120 pounds. "Good job, Gypsy! What a good puppy. And you're not done growing yet."

Puppy? Over a hundred...

Well, I'm still a dog person. I may need to rethink the breed that will go with the name Neema Suellen Grace.

As Tammy and the owner try to regain control over Gypsy, the dog suddenly stops pulling. Sits. Lays to her stomach. Rolls over to her side. Closes her eyes. And starts snoring.

Oh no.

I look in on Malachi.

He blinks sleepy lids at me. Almost grinning, I swear. But he's taken off his front right bootie and he's spread his toes.

All. The. Way. Spread.

Even hooked one of his razor nails on the grate of the door.

And you thought I told him to keep his socks on because he had some sort of fur pattern resembling shoes or socks. And that I was encouraging this kitten to be patient. To wait his turn.

Nope.

I put purple knitted baby booties on my Malachi Maxwell. To cover his toes.

Because every time he spreads his perfectly padded black beans, someone—or something—in direct line of sight of those toes drifts to sleep. Gypsy must've seen Malachi's foot.

Tammy and Zara stare in awe at the massive dog spread in front of the scale. The owner goes frantic, thinking her prized companion has succumbed to a seizure or a stroke, tears streaming. I spin the carrier around and place it on my lap. I unhook Malachi's nail and, trying hard not to go under myself, I open the door, fish around for the lost sock, and replace the bootie without looking directly at his beans. I've done this before, too. Blindly dressing my cat in booties.

"Malachi Maxwell!" I whisper harshly. No one notices, though. Everyone is too worked up about the napping Dane. Tammy yells for Dr. Whitby to come. Zara nudges Gypsy with her toes to no avail.

"Malachi! See what you've done? Keep. Them. On."

How do you reason with a cat?

He readjusts his position, lies flat on his stomach and tucks his two front bootied feet under his breastbone. And blinks.

"—Gypsy. Please. Please. Oh. Oh. Good girl. What was that? What did you do? Are you sleepy today? Huh?" Gypsy struggles to her feet, stumbling like a drunk after a binger. The ruckus moves down the hallway before Doc makes his appearance. Tammy leads the way, shaking her head. Owner Lady gives Gypsy, who's still drowsy but on all fours, a pep talk. Zara brings up the rear, but not before she glances in our direction, her ponytail no longer, black hair spread all over her aqua shoulders.

And gives a look of, well... How could she possibly know what I know? I don't even know what I know, and he's my cat. But it's like she *knows.*

I don't realize it until now, but as soon as that Dane hit the ground, outside of whispering to Malachi, I've been holding my breath. I let out a long sigh, willing my heart to stop pounding, and I wipe my sweaty palms on my jeans, picking up several white and black cat hairs for my efforts.

I turn the carrier full around so Malachi's only view—and his toes' only victim should he ditch the booties again—will be the back of the Formica bench. "Time out, buster. Not cool. Not cool."

A few more patients come. The staff apologizes to me for the wait —they are working Malachi in between the already-scheduled fur babies—and they apologize to me for the Dane scare. I should be the one apologizing to Gypsy.

While I sit here with this cat, praying he keeps his boots on, and watching as other mutts and purebreds fight with the scales and other kitties wail from their carriers, let me tell you how Malachi came to be mine.

It was almost a year ago. July in the Midwest. A triple-digit-check-on-the-elderly kind of heat wave. I was driving home from my own doctor's appointment—allergy testing which all came back negative, that's why I'm here today with Malachi. Something is wrong with my cat...—and I saw a group of middle-school-aged kids gathered and pointing and laughing at something. Then I see fur flying. Black and white fur. Orange and white fur.

The prepubescent monsters were kicking kittens into oncoming traffic. I slam on my brakes and, after a few choice words to society's hope and future and a promise to call the cops if they don't scatter, I find three babies. Pot-bellied and clueless. Scared. No momma in sight. Two were orange and white with crusty blue eyes. The other—Maybelline/Malachi—white and gray tabby. I scooped them up, so fragile I thought I'd surely send them to the Rainbow Bridge with the lightest of touches, and right there in the middle of the road, I emptied a box of emergency car supplies onto the back seat and place the kitties in the box.

Doc Whitby had given me the hard truth that day. He'd have to charge an arm and a leg for these kitties' care and they may not make it. Probably *wouldn't* make it. A rescue free-care shelter was their best bet.

Drove two counties over to the best one I knew of. The same shelter that had rescued and rehabilitated our two ladies waiting at home: Stella Marie and Amara Mino. But this isn't their story. It's Malachi's. The kittens cried all the way for their fur momma that was off who knows where doing who knows what. If she was even alive.

But the Alliance was full up. Waiting room packed. The vet took a peek and said they'd likely not make it a day or two. Make them comfortable. Same thing Doc Whitby had said.

Punch-to-the-gut news. I tell you. Two vets. And I know cats and cases like this are a dime a dozen, but I saw these babies flying into traffic. Evil, evil feet kicking them and making sport of it. I couldn't bear it.

But what do I know of these things? Remember, except for that sixteen-year stint with Cosmo-the-not-quite-a-cat, I'm a full-on dog person.

I drove the whining box of kittens to our farm supply store and bought the most expensive (though not as expensive as humane euthanasia or critical care) replacement cat milk and kitten food I could find. High end, I tell you.

Kitty flea meds.

Kitty de-wormer.

The whole kit-and-kaboodle.

If my husband were around he'd have told me to let it go. Let nature take its course. And if he'd been around, I would've told him I am a force of nature and I'll decide the course.

At least give the poor things a shot.

And we—Minnie, Moose and Maybelline and I—started the long, hot process of de-fleaing, de-worming, and generally providing nourishment in the humid garage, rickety box fans blowing in all directions, a kiddie swimming pool filled with bagged ice to lay against. Did you know cats pant? Triple digit heat wave, I tell you.

It tore my gut in two to keep those furballs outside in the heat. But we had Stella and Amara to think about, and I did have enough sense to know that the babies could be carrying some deadly disease, and I didn't want to expose our grown lady cats to kitty crud. So the babies had to stay in the garage. And every couple of hours I fully expected to find a dead one. Or two.

From the heat. From failure-to-thrive. From a virus or bacteria that bombarded their cells. From injuries unknown. From whatever.

But as the hours and days went on, that didn't happen. They started to perk up. Brighten up. We cleaned them and babied them and let them explore more and more of the backyard. Even the hubs got attached to the time spent and would text me from work to ask how they were getting along.

The girls, Minnie and Moose, thrived. Playing, hopping, hunting bugs and moles, and climbing our giant osage orange trees with the greatest of ease and agility.

Maybelline/Malachi? Not so much.

We'd had them for a few weeks before we realized she was a he. Changed his name. But the entire time, even though he'd done well eating and growing a little, he didn't have the energy of his sisters. Nor the coordination. He fell out of the tree three times. Once I was fast enough to catch him. Twice not so lucky, so we wouldn't let him climb the tree anymore. He didn't seem to mind being grounded and hung at our feet. Sleepy. Lazy.

He'd get tangled in all manner of things. I found him nearly strangled in the hammock net, he'd twisted and twisted until his neck was so tightly bound by the ropes, that he went unconscious in my hands before I could spin him out of the ropey twists. I freed him finally, tapped on his chest and breathed in his face, begging and pleading for him to respond. Tears streaming down my cheeks like Gypsy's owner just moments ago. Totally freaked out.

But Malachi came to and snuggled into my neck.

And that was it. That was the moment.

I'd been commissioned by the hubs to find homes for them, and a kind neighbor wanted the trio for her barn. They'd be great hunters and earn their keep, and in the country, they'd be out of harm's way of traffic and mean-middle-school cretins. But that moment that Malachi regained consciousness in my arms (started his second of nine lives), I knew he wasn't cut out to be a barn cat. Him with his mascara-lined eyes and that crazy little orange freckle on his lip—the shape of a lopsided heart the color of his more-capable sisters.

He didn't have the brain cells for barn life. He'd be dead in a day, breaking his neck from a fall out of the hay loft or nap under a tractor tire. I shuddered to think of it. Probably let the mice nibble him to bits before he'd take one of them out to dinner.

So Malachi Maxwell was adopted. Cleared by Doc Whitby. Introduced to Stella Marie, the fluffy long-haired tabby (who was glad for a friend) and Amara Mino, the diluted calico short hair (who stress ate and protested the intrusion for weeks), and he became mine.

My bitty buddy.

"Malachi Maxwell?" Tammy's ready for us. "Sorry for your wait."

I stand, stretch and after checking that his booties are on, I hand the carrier over to her, praying silently that he keeps his toes covered.

"Let me, Tammy. Gypsy's owner could use a hand." Zara takes the carrier from us. She's pulled her hair up into a tight bun this time. She winks at me.

I'm not sure how to respond. So I just smile at her. "Uh. He, uh. Likes those booties. And they don't weigh much, so…"

She smiles. She *knows*. "I'll keep his socks on. No worries." Malachi and Zara head through the back to the behind-the-scenes kitty scale. She sing-songs to him as they go. "What great purple boots you have, Malachi. I'm quite jealous."

And I know, I know. Purple isn't a very manly color, but it's what I had. I was just lucky I found the knitting needles. I can barely read a pattern. Took it up when I thought I would be animal-less for a while after Spencer Doodles crossed the Rainbow Bridge. Something to relax me. Something low maintenance.

It wasn't relaxing. It was the most frustrating hobby I've ever encountered. I only managed to learn doll booties and a doll-sized bonnet and a loopy hand warmer thing before giving up. Purple was on sale. So little man Malachi Maxwell wears purple.

I wait in the examination room, the hallway door closes behind me, muffling the bustle of two howling bassets in the waiting area. A menacing exam table protrudes from the wall, rib high on me (short girl problems). All my dogs hated the human-assisted hoist onto that table. The counter in the corner holds various innocuous supplies— cotton balls, wooden depressors, swabs. Informative graphics warning pet owners of the dangers of heartworm and feline leukemia plaster the wall around a tiny whiteboard with a blue dry-erase marker tied on a string. A light box waits for x-rays and likely bad news for those whose pets should need that service.

The second door to the exam room—the one that leads to the lab and surgical areas—opens and Zara places Malachi's carrier on the table, the door facing me.

He kept his booties on. What a good boy…

"So what brings you two in today?" She flips through his chart. "He seems to be growing just fine. I take it he's got foot issues?" She glances up at me with that *knowing* look.

I don't even know where to start, so I babble on from the beginning. Taking a big risk. "I think he's got some chemical imbalance or something. I think his feet. Well, I think—"

Doc comes in from the lab door. I change my mind mid-telling and let Doc lead.

"Hey, buddy! Hello Renee." He opens the door to Malachi's carrier. The cat doesn't bother to come out, even when Whitby dangles the end of his stethoscope across the table. Malachi sticks out one purple foot, then the other and peeks around the corner. At the Doc. At me. At Zara. Then pulls his bootied feet back inside and tucks them under his breastbone and blinks in slow motion.

"Well, if that's how it's going to be." Doc unscrews the nuts from around the rim of the carrier and lifts off the top, effectively exposing Malachi without disturbing his catness.

Spoiled rotten, he is. I'd have just pulled him out if it hadn't been for the toe issues. I take a seat to give Doc and the tech room to maneuver. "Let's give you a good look-over." Doc begins his standard of care exam, avoiding the paws, and asks, "So…he's got some nail issues?" He massages Malachi's front foot through the bootie. "He likes to keep his nails out, doesn't he?"

"Well, he does, actually. Most of the time. He's almost a year old and he still can't seem to retract them to walk across carpet or the back of the couch. He's constantly caught in something and just lazes with a foot caught here or there or a dish towel dragging behind him until I untangle his toes."

Doc laughs. Zara giggles and scratches Malachi behind his ears. Mal leans into her hand, and I hear his motor start up.

"So you want him declawed?" Doc asks.

I jump from the bench. "Heavens no!" I nearly call the man a toenail Nazi, but I'd better not ostracize the only vet for miles around. I grab Malachi from his now open-topped carrier.

"Well, there's not much I can—"

"Look, Doc." I say. "I think he's oozing some chemical or something from his feet. I just don't know how to explain it."

"Okay, okay. Let's take a look."

Zara jumps between Doc and me. "Let me help."

While I have Malachi tucked under my armpit, Zara carefully removes his front booties. "Don't look directly at them." I squint. Just in case. I do have to drive home, you know.

Doc feels both front paws and gently turns them to inspect the pads. I brace myself.

Then Doc braces himself, leaning against the table. "Wow. Zara, I don't see anything here, do you? My apologies, Renee. I must not've eaten enough breakfast this morning." He wipes his brow on his shirt sleeve. "Take over, here, Zara? I think he's okay. I think, Renee, you're a dog person. Cats will tell you when they need something…No worries. He'll grow into his toes."

I think Doc is a dog person. I think Doc just got a tiny dose of Malachi's toe jam, and he stumbles through to the lab, shaking his head and patting his cheeks. I've seen that move before after an encounter with Mal's toes.

Zara motions for me to sit. She sits next to me and replaces Malachi's booties. I flip him over like the baby he is, and kiss his lopsided heart freckle. He purrs and closes his eyes, four purple paws relaxed and undercover. "You're impossible," I whisper. Zara hears.

"Start from the beginning. Tell me everything." She pats me on the leg. I notice a freckle on her wrist, a not-quite-oval. More like, well… Like a lopsided heart the color of Malachi's birth sisters. "I promise I'll believe you."

So I tell her. About the sleepiness—mine, not Malachi's. About the sisters going to the farm. About, well. Strange things around the house in general.

She grins, a strand of black hair brushes her cheek. She reaches that freckled hand up to push it back, and the thing—that lopsided heart thing—glowed. She rubs Malachi's belly. "Renee! Congratulations! You've rescued a Mag-Line. I knew it as soon as Gypsy hit the floor in the waiting room."

"A what?"

"A Mag-Line. Half Magic. Half Feline. Well, in Malachi's instance, he may be just one-quarter. But you were wise to do the bootie thing. His dosing is relatively light. But he could grow into it…" Zara says all of this like she's done it a hundred times.

Cat puts people to sleep? Oh, no worries. You've got yourself a standard-issue Mag-Line. Cat wears booties? Good job raising that Mag-Line, Renee. She stands and readies the carrier, screwing the top back on so I can place Malachi inside. We close the door. He barely woke up to reposition himself. Nothing bothers that cat. He and Zara have a lot in common.

Freckles and all.

She digs into her scrub pocket and pulls out a card. An orange glittery emblem in the top right corner matches my cat's lip freckle. And the one on my vet tech's wrist.

"We've been seeing an increase in these cases. It's contagious, you know. The Mag-Line's magic. Any problems with your other cats?"

I don't even know where to begin. There's a number and an address on the card. One county over. "What are you telling me? Contagious?" Now, I find myself to be a reasonable human being most of the time. Grounded. Even was reasonable enough to leave Malachi and his malnourished sisters in the hot garage while they convalesced so our other cats wouldn't catch mange or fleas or something… But this? Magic?

"Only rarely. Only if there's a genetic link. Only with other felines, so you won't sprout magical toes." Zara laughs at her own joke. I'm not finding any of this funny. Neither is my jaw, which hangs in a semi-permanent open state. "There's a support group for owners. Bring Malachi. Being with the older cats will help him tame down and not use his, well, use his toes on you." Zara giggles again and uses a finger to scratch my bitty buddy's head through the carrier door.

"Call me anytime, Renee. Day or night. We'll get you and Malachi through this." She hands me the carrier. "Better settle up out front before the next wave of pooches comes through. Tammy wouldn't understand. Doc, either, if all of the canines hit the ground in snores. They're dog people anyway." I'm speechless. Zara opens the hall door for me and I walk through a wave of confusion to the front desk. Tammy's trying to fix the be-quiet candle that Gypsy knocked off.

I hand her my credit card, careful to keep Malachi's door away from curious onlookers of any species. She swipes it. Says something about a followup appointment for shots. Zara's shaking her head at me behind Tammy with a finger to her lips.

Secret.

Magic cats. Contagious ones.

Well, that explains it. If this is something that can be explained.

Purple booties.

I drive home. Ten minutes. We live close. Good thing. I don't think I could handle a long drive after the news I got.

I get through the front door and place the carrier on the counter and open the door. Malachi stretches out. He kept his booties on. He jumps down and disappears down the hallway.

My ladies come to greet me.

Stella Marie. Her long tabby coat shiny and flowing. Her bushy tail tucked carefully into that purple loopy hand warmer I'd made even before she came home from the rescue. I dug it out after I knitted Malachi's booties. You don't want her to brush up against you with that tail of hers. Trust me. Learned that the hard way. But this isn't Stella's tale of her tail. Not today. I give her a head scratch, she leans back into it, her little snaggle teeth grinning up at me. And off she goes, passing Amara.

Amara Mino. It took her a few days to get used to the bonnet. Purple. I'd only bought one color of yarn. I cut a slit for her left ear. Her right ear is the troublesome one. It already had a nick in it from a previous injury. The first time it happened with her, she'd flicked her little ear and well... But this isn't Amara's ear-tip tale, either. Not today.

Today is about the realization that I've done gone and rescued a Mag-Line that infected my ladies with his magical toe ooze.

One never had to worry about this with dogs.

And now here the three cats—magically infected ones at that—sit, waiting patiently in their purple knitted ensembles for wet tuna food from the can. Booties on my little man. Tail scarf and bonnet on my ladies.

Maybe this is normal. I take the card Zara gave me and examine it. I mean, support groups and everything. And we're not even near a big city. No one told me raising cats could come with this risk. I thought the furniture scratching and the midnight prowling and the litter box issues would be handful enough. Maybe this is the new cat-owner normal. Maybe not.

But what do I know? I'm a dog person.

LEGACY

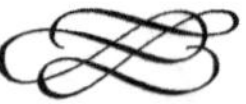

When her grandmother passes, Sandra realizes just how little she knows about her extended family. When an unexpected gift arrives for her the night of the funeral, Sandra realizes just how little any of them knew about her granny.

"Legacy" is the recipient of Writers of the Future Honorable Mention in 2019.

Sandra stood next to her mother and watched as dozens of people lined the perimeter of the viewing room at Sandusky Funeral Home. The line snaked from the end of Elizabeth Rose Gallaway's casket all the way out the front door and onto the sidewalk. Intermingled with strangers were family members she hadn't seen for quite some time. Some faces she recognized, but the names and relationships escaped her.

"You should know your family. Family is everything," Granny chided Sandra repeatedly when she would interrupt one of Granny's gossip sessions to explain that she really didn't know who the old woman was talking about.

Sandra tugged at the neckline of her black dress and pushed the sleeves up as high as they could go. The small funeral home's air conditioning could barely keep up with the August swelter; the bodies and breath filling the room taxed the system to the brink. She wished she could kick off her shoes like her little cousins did as soon as they arrived at the viewing, but she didn't think it was appropriate, and that would mean standing barefoot on the matted blue and yellow paisley carpet.

Occasionally, Sandra would leave the receiving line to browse through the cards stuck in the flower arrangements, attached to the afghans or dangling from the dozen or so windchimes that people sent ahead to the funeral home. The staff brought out extra stands for some of the arrangements. Throws woven with sentimental poems graced either side of the bathroom doors.

I'll never forget what you did for me.

Liz was a lifesaver. May she rest in peace.

There's no one left to fill her shoes.

Heaven gained an angel.

The cards went on and on. Most of the senders were unfamiliar to Sandra.

Granny was right. Sandra really didn't know anything about her relatives and probably never will now that Granny was gone. Her parents certainly never spoke of these vaguely familiar people now gushing condolences, hugs and, "I remember when Liz..."

"Liz," as many called Granny, was probably the smartest person Sandra knew. Not in the sense of book smart. She never went to her grandmother for algebra help or—heaven help her—dating advice. But Granny always *knew* things. And if she didn't, she would slip on her gold and blue spectacles, pull out her ancient phone directory, and find a number to call that would have the answer.

Sandra returned to her mother's side to see just as many people around the walls as there were twenty minutes ago. Mom hugged them and teared up with some, turning to face the oak casket lined with pink and white satin. Sandra didn't like looking at Granny. Without her old glasses dangling from the blue chain around her neck, Granny didn't seem complete. The old glasses were lost when Granny was transferred to the nursing home a couple weeks ago.

Sandra wished she could retreat to the front row of red fabric-covered chairs set up in the middle of the room, but they were either taken or stained with coffee or tears.

Another couple of hours and, finally, the last visitor hugged and cried with the family. As the funeral director started closing doors and turning off lights, Sandra stretched her arms high over her head and noticed makeup and tear smudges covering the shoulders of her dress. Perfumes and colognes had rubbed off, too, and a headache was starting at the back of her neck from stress and mingled scents.

The family—Mom, two aunts and their children and spouses, and Sandra—faced the casket for the last time. The lady director asked if her mother was ready. Mom nodded a tired yes. And the lid was closed forever on Elizabeth Rose Gallaway.

They were in the parking lot when an overweight, suited man jogged up to them, slightly out of breath.

"I'm so very sorry, but which one of you is Sandra?"

Sandra startled a bit. No one through this ordeal paid any specific attention to her, or her cousins for that matter. "Me." She stepped toward the unfamiliar gentleman. He reached up to swat a mosquito with one hand, nearly knocking off his glasses. He held a small cardboard box in his other hand. He straightened his glasses on his nose, and Sandra caught a shimmer of green sparkle from the edge of his frames. The heat and stress were getting to her.

"I have instructions that granddaughter, Sandra Rose, be the recipient. Here you go, young lady. Truly sorry for your loss." The sweaty man handed her the box, turned and jogged down the sidewalk in the opposite direction.

"What is this?" she asked her mom.

"I have no idea, sweetheart." They slid into the family's SUV and cranked up the AC.

Sandra's hair blew in the vent as the cool air dried the sweat. She turned the box over in her hands.

"Well, you gonna open it?" Dad prodded.

"Maybe she left you something because you're the oldest grandchild," Mom said.

"I didn't think there was anything else." Sandra stared at the box in her lap. After Granny died, the aunts had split up all the possessions from her small country home. There had been no squabbling like you hear about in some families after a death. Maybe because there wasn't much to fight over. Aside from modest furnishings and a few decorations, Granny had mostly books, vintage McCall's and newspapers from the '40s. When it was Sandra's turn to pick something as a memento, she had gladly chosen Granny's 1957 paperback phone directory. The tattered, retro book was a standing joke in the family, and Sandra wanted to remember Granny that way. Ornery and wise— not how sick she was in the end.

"You won't know unless you open it."

The fatigue of the evening settled to her bones, and Sandra teared up for the first time since she heard that Granny had passed. She hated crying in front of her parents. The last time, when Mom had found Sandra sobbing on her bed after flunking her final exam in Chemistry, she had offered to find Sandra a therapist. Mom didn't know how to handle Sandra's teenage mood swings.

But now she couldn't hold back the tears. After she recovered, she said, "I want to wait until I'm alone, I think."

"Well, you'll show us later, then, yes?"

"Yeah, Mom."

IN THE SAFETY of her room, Sandra changed out of the stale funeral dress into a tank and shorts and flopped onto her bed. The small, white box sat on the end of the bed and she stared at it and let the tears come again. She reached for the phone directory that she'd left on her nightstand and caressed the cover.

The old book had yellowed with age and the page edges were brittle with little slivers of paper missing here and there. The cover still held its '50s charm. A mustard yellow hand receiver with a coiled cord was pictured down the right edge. The spine's edge had a pale green background with white cursive lettering spelling out *Telephone Directory.* Halfway down the cover, in black, was *Sandusky and Nearby Points* and *The United Telephone Company of Pennsylvania.* Granny moved from Pennsylvania to Indiana decades ago after Gramps passed. Thus, one-third of the standing family joke. That she would keep such a useless thing for so long.

Sandra opened the book to the middle pages and leafed through, careful not to chip away any more of the fragile edges. The second third of the joke was that the pages were all blank. Not a single printed word, phone number, name or address was listed in this phone book. A printing press error, no doubt. But time after time, Granny would put on her gold reading spectacles, pull the directory from the top of her Maytag fridge and "look somethin' up right quick." With earnest concentration, she would examine the blank pages until she came up with a phone number, grinning from ear to ear.

Sandra rested her head back on the headboard, closed her eyes and remembered the last part of the joke. Well, more one-hundred percent mystery than one-third joke. The phone numbers that Granny had pulled from those blank pages were always right. No matter how obscure the facts that she was "lookin' up," no matter where that one neighbor from twenty years ago may be now, no matter.

The numbers were always right.

And they were always in service.

And the person on the other end of those numbers always had the answer to whatever vague, concrete or otherwise crazy question or conundrum anyone posed to Granny.

Sandra returned the book to the nightstand, leaving the pages open, and smiled. She'd once asked Granny what kind of roses she should plant for her agricultural project. Granny smiled, put on her gold spectacles, and consulted the phone book. She gave Sandra a ten-digit phone number, which Sandra called while rolling her eyes.

The man who'd answered was an award-winning gardener in southern Indiana who took grand prize at the state fair for his Carefree Sunshine bush with blossoms six inches across.

Or the time Sandra's cat kept throwing up hairballs all over her white bedspread. She told Granny of her frustrations. With a wink and a grin, out came the spectacles. Out came the directory. Another ten-digit number. This time, the lady who answered was a veterinarian in Cincinnati specializing in feline digestive health. She was happy to give Sandra advice on the matter.

At a family reunion several years ago, one of the aunts had brought a 100-page blank composition notebook. The group had sat around, eating fried chicken and reminiscing about other times when Granny had known what to do, or rather, who to call. The family filled all but fifteen of those pages with similar instances, and they probably could have filled the rest, but Granny put a stop to it.

"I help who I can help. No sense in dwelling on it like this. Unless, of course, you're gonna read that at my funeral for the eulogy!" They put the book away, but decided to call her Granny Google behind her back.

After many conversations and the occasional heated debate, the family came to the general conclusion that Granny had a photographic memory. That she spent time memorizing the Yellow Pages from the tristate area out of current directories that she hid some-where, and the rest was just for show.

Sandra scooted to the middle of her bed and toyed with the edges of the white cardboard. She slid the lipped closure out of the slot and opened the lid.

Inside was a brown envelope the size of an index card and a generic-looking black eyeglass pouch. She opened the envelope, trying not to rip the whole thing. The envelope and the bi-folded paper it held were as brittle as the directory pages. She unfolded it. Scrolled in her grandmother's shaky cursive she read:

Sandra, my dear love. Carry on the Legacy. May 2016.

She set the note on her pillow and removed the black glasses case. She'd not seen it before. She tipped it upside down and gasped. Granny's spectacles slid from the case and onto her lap. She tossed the case to the floor and gingerly picked up the frames. Tears flowed again and she held the folded glasses up to her face and sobbed. The faint odor of Granny's VO5 hair oil hung on the frame.

She swung open the earpieces and examined the details. Most of the frame was gold. The earpieces were inlaid with pale green vines and the brightest blue butterflies that seemed to flit and twirl along the sides. She brought the glasses up to eye level and peered through. Her volleyball trophies and photos of prom on the far wall blurred through the lenses.

Sandra moved back to the head of the bed, placed the glasses on the opened directory and reached for the note.

May 2016.

If the date was correct, Granny wrote this over a year before she got sick. But how did the glasses end up with the sweaty guy from the funeral?

She glanced toward the nightstand and saw something shimmer green through the lenses. She first thought it was her small table lamp shining through the glass onto the page, but when she looked closer, she lost her breath.

She pulled the book onto her bed and held the spectacles above the blank page.

She caught the shimmer again.

She put the glasses on her face, way down on her nose like her grandmother had done hundreds of times before and gazed through them at the book.

A ten-digit number floated off the page, carried by pale green vines and bright blue flittering butterflies in three-dimensional resolution. She reached out to touch the number, and the image bent around the tips of her fingers.

She turned the page. The number briefly disappeared, then reappeared once the page was set still in her lap. She turned another with the same results.

She looked up through the lenses at the wall across the room. Trophies blurred. The photos were a mess of nondescript heads and backgrounds.

She looked down again where butterflies and the same ten digits greeted her.

She lost time staring at the image, playing with the insects at her fingertips. Finally, she traded book and glasses for her cell phone.

She carefully entered the ten numbers, pressed send, and held the phone to her ear with a trembling hand.

"Hello, sweet Sandra. It's your Granny."

STAY IN TOUCH!

BAPAUL.COM

Take a glimpse into B.A. Paul's writing journey, including the ups and downs of managing family, "real jobs," ducks in wobbling rows, and chasing down her Little Miss Muse. New blog posts go up Mondays, with the first Monday of the Month reserved for a free fiction short story available on the blog for a limited time.

Newsletter Signup!
Click here to sign up for the newsletter and receive a free exclusive short story!
Get the latest release information, author updates, and exclusive content.

ABOUT THE AUTHOR

Beth enjoys chucking words into sentences then standing back to see what magic—or mayhem—falls out, crafting tales in mystery, sci-fi, fantasy, and general "slice of life" fiction. She couldn't accomplish this without the help of her tutu-clad Little Miss Muse and Trudi the Concrete Office Goose, who's partial to superhero capes.

Her stories have appeared in multiple publications, including Pulphouse Fiction Magazine and Ellery Queen Mystery Magazine, and in multiple fiction anthologies. She's received several Honorable Mentions from Writers of the Future. Her lighthearted blog peeks into the writing life as she pokes fun at herself and her circus of a life.

Follow the antics of Little Miss Muse and Trudi, read Beth's blog (she might have burned down her kitchen last week), and discover the stories at bapaul.com.

ALSO BY B. A. PAUL

Short Story Collections

Spunk and Spice, Volumes 1 and 2: A Collection of six short stories celebrating timeless wit and wisdom.

Out There, Volumes 1 and 2: A Collection of six short sci-fi and speculative tales.

Mystery Minutes, Volumes 1 and 2: Six short mystery stories

All the Feels, Volumes 1, 2, and 3: Collections of inspiring short stories

Just a Tick of Whimsy, Volumes 1 and 2: Collections of fantasy shorts.

Hijacked Holidays: Definitely not your warm-and-fuzzy winter tales.

Dark Minds: Toe-curling twisted mysteries.

Blog Compilations: Slices of the writing life with lots of laughs and bumps in the road.

Life Along the Way

Life All Over Again

Novels

Triage

Young Adult (or Young at Heart) Books

Switch: Book 1 in the Oliver Andrews Trilogy

9 781964 800004